B. W. N
By Nathan \

To Kyle, for a long list of inspiration.

Chapter I

"So, what is it again?'

"It's said to be the most powerful weapon on Earth."

"But, it's just a young boy."

"Looks can deceive us all, Ms. Sword. It is always how something looks that can make something seem safe. This is the deadliest thing Earth has ever seen."

"Well, I guess it makes sense that it's in Area 51, then."

This is the first conversation I heard when I awoke. It's a strange feeling, becoming conscious for the first time. It's like waking from a dream you never remembered entering. Except that this slumber, I knew for a fact, had lasted for fourteen years, constantly having every bit of knowledge gathered from the planets around us being poured into my vast sea of intellect.

My name is Victor Forte. Well, that's the name I took when I woke up. My true identification is "B. W. M. D." or "Biological Weapon of Mass Destruction." How true this is because, in the information I had received while I was asleep, I learned that I was meant to be the most dangerous thing alive. But, that was not the purpose that I wanted for myself.

Anyway, when I woke up, I saw the two people that had discussed my existence walk away. A middle height man and a shorter woman. I wanted to follow them, but there was a wall of something in my way. I touched it and instantly felt weaker. I thought nothing of it until I felt a sharp pain in my hand. As I drew back my hand, I noticed the second strange thing about my being.

The tank was filled with some sort of liquid, yet I could breathe easily, implying that I could easily also be amphibious. I wondered how many pros and cons there were to my being.

Looking around my tank, I looked straight up. The lid was made out of a different material than the rest of my prison. I swam up, careful not to touch the wall. I lifted my left hand and pressed against it. I felt another decrease in energy. *Stupid!* I thought. *If they were going to make something so deadly, why put it in something it can easily get out of?*

Taking another glance before resuming my slumber, maybe to keep myself busy with some long algebraic division or with a copy of Shakespeare's ***A Midsummer's Night Dream***, I noticed the floor was made of yet another material. I thought that it would be yet another dead-end until I noticed where my bare feet were. On the floor. On the painless, smooth floor. This was the mistake of a life time for the architect.

I flipped upside down and tapped the floor, thinking that maybe the drain I felt in my strength was only caused when my arms came in contact with this substance. That was not the case, which meant that I could get out this way. If only I had a knife or a sword. Even a paper clip would do. I floated there, eyes shut, thinking what I could possibly do when I felt my hand start to burn. I thought this may be the result of the liquid I was in (which, by the way, I discovered was acidic mercury), so I ignored it until it was almost unbearable.

Opening my eyes, I saw that where my normal, human-like hand once was, sat a clawed hand. I tapped it with my other hand and instantly drew blood from it. However, this cut was short lived as I saw new skin creep over the wound. Both the claw and the instant healing of my hand took me by surprise.

Tapping the floor with that giant claw, I punctured it. I drew a circle and pushed it down. Somehow, the liquid stayed in the tank, even as I pulled myself through my makeshift porthole. As I made contact with the air outside, I felt a shift in the pull of gravity. So, I was grown upside down, maybe so that all of the knowledge I gained would stay in my head. This was highly unlikely, but it didn't hurt to consider all of the options.

I placed the circle of material back, bent it in a way it would hold still, and started to walk through my new metal world.

I saw that I was in a giant room with no windows. There were giant metal machines with purposes I could name alphabetically, chronologically, or chronologically alphabetical if I wished to. There were also other tubes of what could possibility become more B.W.M.D.'s.

Walking further down, I chanced upon a closet of spare outfits. This was lucky because, looking down; I noticed that the only clothing I had were a pair of boxers. Seeing the inventory of the wardrobe, I settled on a simple blue shirt, black athletic pants, and a grey, ratty sweatshirt. A simple outfit, but it beat walking around almost naked all the time.

I heard footsteps coming toward me. I knew that they must be guards or scientists because, logically speaking, who else would be in this facility. I searched through all knowledge I had on myself, closing my eyes as I watched all the information run in front of my eyes.

After about three seconds, I found something that may be of some use: I could blend into my surroundings as long as I made absolutely no movements. It sounded simple enough, so I stepped outside the closet, lodged myself on a stack of boxes, and sat still, breathing long, silent breaths.

Walking past me were two men: Peter Wily, aka "Alpha," and Dmitri Recoil, or "Omega." They were part of the special team, put into action in major dilemmas. Peter may be the right man to lead the team, but he couldn't stop Dmitri's habit of getting drunk constantly. Dmitri started up a conversation, in an Irish accent that he developed after too many shots of, well, anything except air. No, scratch that. He could probably have gotten drunk off of the air, also.

"How long has it been since our last mission?"

"Ten Years."

"Why do we still work here, huh? I have a wife and two beautiful children that I can only see two days a month. Nothing goes wrong here. We're almost never needed."

"You and I both know that we have to be here as long as there is a possibility that the B.W.M.D. can get out. I'll tell you what, if you can go the next week without drinking, I will personally make sure that you can get a week off a month."

"You would do that for me?"

"Or you could just quit," I said, shifting so I was now visible. Alpha and Omega turned towards me with wide eyes. They aimed their guns at me, but I simply smiled, knowing the bullets were useless due to the fact that I can stop them in hundreds of ways. You can't be deadly without being able to stop some of the things trying to kill you. They opened fire, only to have their bullets stop in mid-air and drop to the ground.

Hopping from the boxes, I ran past them towards the nearest door. This led to an experimental aircraft hangar. It was filled with technology that should not have existed in the twenty-first century. This included Mache XXX jets, jetpacks, and other types of flying aids. I was searching for something that could help me escape when I heard an extremely high pitched screech. I clasped my hands to my ears, the sound knocking me to the floor.

The rest of the Special Team, Amelia Waits (Beta), Vladimir Runcoff (Gamma), Jeremy Stopper (Epsilon), George Stovepipe (Delta), and Dmitri came rushing in, brandishing their guns with the same excitement of a five-year-old at Christmas. This was most likely because they hadn't had any excitement since the "Second Roswell," but that's a story for another time. Peter was nowhere to be found, but I wasn't worried about him right now. I was a little preoccupied with myself.

Walking in, a look of pride on his face, was Mr. Jonathan Tell, the head scientist of the B.W.M.D. production, and the owner of one of the voices I heard when I awoke. Behind him was a very frightened Donna Sword, his assistant.

Jonathan held his arms out to the sides as if to give me a hug. "At last, my son has awakened!"

"I'm not your son or anyone else's who happens to work here. I was grown in a tank, as I'm sure you know."

"Oh, you think so, Victor?"

"How did you... Wait a minute. You pre-planned everything that happened here?"

"Everything up until you awoke and escaped. I know exactly how much knowledge you possess and how many abilities you currently have. So, be a good boy and go with the Specials to the lab so we can check to make sure everything went alright. I don't want anything to be wrong with the newest member of my family."

The Special team started to close in on me. I knew that I had one escape and one only, and it involved the fact that half of the team was alcoholic. I stretched my arm out, point past Jonathan, and yelled, "Whiskey!" That did it. The half that was alcoholic ran over Jonathan in an attempt to get to the imaginary drink. The other half chased them down, also running over their most likely enraged employer. In the chaos, I slipped away and ran down the hall.

I could hear more and more guards and scientists come running my way. I knew I was getting close to the exit, but I veered to the left into a room that consisted of explosives. I slammed and locked the door and started looking for something that would make the best escape.

The Flood and Gomorrah? No, The Flood was a bomb the created a shift in the atmosphere the causes forty day long rainstorms, even indoors. Gomorrah had a similar effect but it created flaming projectiles from the dust in the air. Fire and water cancel each other out. What else was there?

Gaia Shift and "Mountains"? Gaia Shift caused a giant crack to form wherever the bomb landed. "Mountains" does what the name implies: creates mountains on impact. These two, again, would cancel each other out. There had to be something here that would help.

I heard the door start to break at the hinges, signaling that I was running out of time. Eventually, I just reached out for three materials and decided to make them work. One was Acidic Mercury, something like me who has been soaking in it since "birth" could stand it, but the acid is one of the fastest-acting in the world. The second was the Moment, a bomb that created a shift in time that lasted for days to weeks at a time. Well, in the user's time, anyway. The last was The Flood. This actually was a good combination.

They had just about knocked down the door before I had finished my bomb. I attached the Moment to The Flood by ripping a little off of each and jamming them together, and then covered them both in acidic mercury. The shells were holding, so maybe the acid had no effect on them. It didn't matter though, the door was almost down. When they got through, I started my speech.

"Why, hello there. My name is Victor Forte, the B.W.M.D. that has been growing in your basement for the past few years. I would like to introduce you to my new friend, the Doomsday I. This little baby is equipped with your precious Moment and Flood. All coated in Acidic Mercury. Let me out or this goes up." They parted like the red sea for Moses. I waltzed out, grabbing one person's gun bag, which I knew had held more dangerous things than Doomsday I.

The pack on my back, I set out for the world outside, "accidently" spilling a lot of Acidic Mercury behind me. I was now assured an escape. With a smile, I finally left my prison, setting out for the journey of a lifetime.

Chapter II

I finally left the facility and stepped out into the sunlight. The world around me now was completely different from the one I awoke in. Due to my knowledge of geography, I knew I saw in Las Vegas, Nevada. I found it ironic that, while most people would do anything to get here, I was trying to leave.

I searched through the knowledge of myself again and discovered that I can run at inhumanly high speeds with little need for rest. I decided to try heading north, just to see a part of the country before they found a way out of the hangar. I had nowhere in mind, so I just ran north. No plans, no anticipatable obstacles, I could probably do just about anything that my heart desired.

After running for about thirty minutes, which was roughly four hundred miles for me, I came to an excessively large forest in Kentucky. I decided to stop here for the night, half because I was tired, half because I wanted to have a first-hand experience of one. I mean, I've slept for fourteen years in a vat of one of the most deadly substances on Earth. Why not have changes of scenery in my...

I want to say "life" in that spot, but is that really the right word? I mean, to be alive is, to my understanding, to be born, to live, and to die. I, on the other hand, was *grown* in a vat of acid. I may be living now, but will I ever die? Is it possible that the ability to die would contradict me being the world's deadliest weapon? Until this was resolved, I exchanged "life" with "existence."

I was still pondering these questions when I heard a scream come from the forest. It sounded like a girl, most likely aged at twelve years. I ran in towards it and, twenty yards in, I found exactly that. She looked about thirteen years old, actually, but other than that, she had golden hair and her eyes were, oddly, of matching color. She was screaming because she of the beasts that were attacking her.

They looked mostly human in form, wearing simple black, hooded garments. These humanoids are natives to the planet Beta-Kai, which sat at the edge of the Galmorian galaxy. They looked like humans in every way except for one simple, yet very noticeable, detail, which I revealed as I ran up and pulled one of their hoods off: their mouths were four times too large. I exactly what they were then: Howlers. These were perhaps the most deadly creatures to me because of their ability. I'll give you one guess as to why their mouths are that big.

Instantly, I jumped in front of the girl. She seemed to be shocked at the fact that someone had heard her. She jumped a little higher when I brought out my claws. I whispered to her, "Get up that tree," nodding towards a large sugar oak that was close by. She obliged, quite quickly actually. Almost too quickly.

Turning back to the Howlers, I was met with a blast of sound. It knocked me into a nearby tree. I quickly took in my advantages and disadvantages. The Howlers always traveled in groups of five to fifty members. This group had seven, which meant that this was most likely a rogue groups. Howlers also came equipped with a "built-in" base cannon, a weapon that shot sound waves amplified so high that they can be shot with destructive force. Things looked bad for me here...

Until I remembered that Howlers always attacked as one, and always at the same general target, usually in the same general direction. This was my advantage. Another really good one was the fact that Howlers only have power when they can screech. And to be able to screech, they need their heads. So, that meant my only real offence was... oh, no.

As much as I hated it, I still had no choice. Immediately, I flipped over the Howlers, taking two heads with me. The feeling was horrible, their blood running down my hand, but I would worry about it later. There were still five left, and they had me in their sights. But, there was no way that I was going to... do that again.

I stood in my place and waited for the Howlers to shout at me again. I knew one technique that had an interesting effect on Howlers. They were just as deadly to themselves as they were to others. But, since they were only a group of rogues, I highly doubted that they knew that about themselves.

Right before they shouted, I jumped into the center of their newly formed circle. They all turned inwards, the only exception to their "attack in one direction" rule. I stood there until the last second, and then ducked as far down as I could go.

And that was the end of it. None of them were left standing. The seven dead creatures spooked me a little, maybe because I had a hand in the deaths. I looked at my blood stained claw and shuttered. I watched it turn back into a claw and the blood went away, but it didn't matter. I could still feel it there, sticking to my skin. I didn't want to dwell on it any longer. I called up to the girl to come down. When she did, she threw her arms around me.

"Thank you, so much," she said, crying a little. "You have no idea what that meant to me. They had been hunting me down for weeks."

"You're welcome. But enough about Howlers. I want you tell me who and what you are. I know that you are not human, fully anyway."

"You have to tell who you are first."

"Fair enough. My name is Victor Forte. I'm... special, in a way."

"In what way?"

After taking a while to think if I should tell her about myself or not, I decided it wouldn't make a difference if I did. "I wasn't born like others are. I was grown. I am the product of someone wanting to make an unimaginable weapon. I am a B.W.M.D. or a 'Biologic Weapon of Mass Destruction.'"

"Wow, that's amazing. My name is Natalie Star. I'm from... uh... I can't remember."

"Really?"

"Nope, sorry. I guess I can't keep my end of the bargain."

"Well, maybe I can help you. I am traveling around. You know, getting to know my world a little better until I'm taken from it. We may cross some of the places you were once. Maybe that will spark your memory."

"Thank you."

We walked through the woods, coming to a clearing where we could rest for the night. I built a small fire to keep us warm, though I wasn't sure how effective it would be in late November. Natalie ran off to get more firewood while I hunted for our supper and thought to myself.

Why were her eyes gold? From the knowledge I had on humans, gold wasn't a natural eye color. And why did her name sound so familiar? Thinking on this, I suddenly remembered one of my dreams for my time growing in the vat. I once saw a list, but of what, I couldn't remember. Most of the list was blurry except for four names: Peter Wily, Tia Solaris, Natalie Star, and my own. I knew that Peter and Tia were not married, let alone have met, at that time, but could that have changed? And, why would it have a supposed family on it if the list didn't feel like it was just a census.

I was awoken from my thoughts as I fell into a small stream. Instead of getting out, I waited for the water to settle and looked at my reflection. I was a little tan, had a high-set nose, slightly large ears...

And gold eyes and hair. This startled me at first, but then I thought a bit. Was it possible that Natalie was like me? But that wasn't possible because both Peter and Tia, who was a scientist, were not like me. Or were they? So, what connection did the four of us have? This was getting almost too strange to bear, even for someone like me, who shouldn't exist in the first place.

Again, my thoughts were interrupted, but this time, it was not by my falling into the water, but by footsteps. I held completely still, turning invisible yet again. I heard voices.

"That creature must be out here somewhere," one voice said.

"You've said that at every place we've stopped so far. And every time you've said it, you've been wrong!"

I couldn't believe it. Those were the voices of Jeremy and Vladimir. The special team must have gotten out... some...

DANG IT! I mentally yelled at myself. There were several escapes that they could have used. For one, Acidic Mercury is one of the fastest working acids on the planet, but that means the effect is also short lived. How could I have possibly missed that fact? Another escape for them is the fact that they still had experimental teleports. I need to work more on my observation skills.

Vladimir retaliated with, "That's because every place we've materialized in, we've been right behind him."

"So why don't you look at where he's been and calculate where he'll go? Will that go against everything you stand for, O Lord of the Teleported?"

"Because… because…"

"Because that would mean I'm right and you're wrong, yet again?" I had to laugh at that burn. Vladimir was never the brightest or most observant. Jeremy, however, was both the most observant of the six and had the greatest sense of humor. The latter usually got him in trouble with Alpha a lot.

"Shut up! Now, let's get going. We're going to go to the next best possible place he could be."

"*I'm* selecting the coordinates this time. If you keep going on like this, we'll make Antarctica in no time!" I heard a faint *zap* and then complete silence. I have to say, I am amazed that the two of them were not killed in the process of transporting their atoms across long distances in a split second.

I headed back towards the make-shift campsite, empty handed from my "thrilling" hunt. I noticed that Natalie was already asleep, huddled close to a nearby tree. I smiled as I silently walked over to her. She looked kind of cold, lying out here with nothing but a short sleeve T-shirt and shorts. I took off my sweatshirt, draped it over her, and then sat on the other side of the fire.

Why did I do that? I was supposed to be instant death to most, so why should I take pity on a defenseless girl? Better yet, why had I disobeyed orders back at the facility? And, why had I felt horrified at the fact that I had killed something, even if I was meant for that very purpose. Perhaps I wasn't geared to be a cold-hearted killer. Maybe, during my growth, I had developed free will.

Or, maybe it was because I felt a strong connection with this girl.

■■

I woke up at the crack of dawn. Natalie was still asleep, so I decided to go have another attempt at hunting. This time, I had more luck and brought back two fair sized turkeys. I skinned them, cleaned them, and had them over the newly rekindled fire before Natalie became conscious again. She stretched and sat up, smiling at me.

"Good morning. I see you found breakfast."

"Yeah, I had more luck this time. They're almost done, so why don't eat some then we can be on our way. I don't want to stay here any longer than is necessary."

I took one turkey and gave her the other. I didn't realize how hungry I was. But it made sense, considering I had slept for fourteen years straight without anything except Acidic Mercury for substance. I must have set a world record for killing, preparing, and eating a turkey. Take that, participants of the human custom of Thanksgiving!

I looked up for my bones to see Natalie finishing off her own turkey. We both must have been starving. I laughed at this. After a few seconds, she joined in on my laughter. We laughed the entire time we cleaned up the "campsite" and left the woods.

We are *a couple of misfits,* I said to myself. The B.W.M.D. and the girl who forgot, together, we were a strange pair. Little did we know things could only get stranger for us.

Chapter III

After running for about an hour or so (well, I was running and Natalie was on my back), we came to a small town in Ohio. It was a simple village, full of friendly people, a few restaurants, a shop, and several houses. It was at the little shop that we discovered a dark secret that was harbored in this little haven.

As we were looking around the small shop, I saw a young man, maybe my age sitting at one of the tables. He had his nose in a small sketchbook, periodically writing or drawing something in it. Something felt strange about him, like he emitted a certain power. As we left, I felt him gaze at us.

Once outside, I turned to Natalie. "Did you see that boy in there?"

"The one with the book? Yeah. When I looked at him, I felt like... like I should know him."

"Someone from your past maybe?"

"Perhaps, but it's too hard to say for certain. I would like to know more about him though."

Just then, an old man walked up to us. He was about four foot two, with pure white hair that stuck out from under his light brown, almost tan hat, which he pulled over his face as he approached. His beard fell to about mid-breast. He was wearing a simple, brown trench coat. His voice was gruff and hoarse, like he had shouted for years. His tone certainly sounded like he had.

"Are you two new in town?"

"Why do you want to know?" I asked in an equally mean voice. I didn't like this man for some reason.

"I was just wondering if whether or not you knew to stay away from that boy in there."

"Why?" Natalie asked, in a puzzled tone.

"The story goes that this town is not meant to be here. It only exists because of that young boy."

"What?"

"Supposedly, that boy came here one day with a group of raiders. Miles and miles he traveled with the, tormented into supplying them with whatever their hearts desired.

"Then, the day they reached here, he decided he had enough. Wanting a haven from their constant harassment, he picked up his sketchbook and drew the first house in this town. He ran in and boarded the door shut. When his tormentors attempted to enter, he drew a giant iron guardian to protect him. The giant killed the men and tended to the boy.

"Feeling lonely, he drew more houses and people, keeping his power a secret to all but one, my ancestor. He was the first person he ever drew; He knew that he is extremely deadly. From that day on, that boy, much older than he looks, had haunted this town."

Natalie and I shared a glance. Then, looking back at the man, I said, almost with a laugh, "You're kidding, right?"

"Just stay away from him!" With that, he hobbled off, using a cane that we hadn't noticed earlier. We turned to go elsewhere when we noticed the boy right behind us.

"Leave my domain, now! You do not belong here," he yelled at us. He took out his book and wrote something down. Tearing out the page, he handed it to us and yelled again, "Leave!" He then ran off.

I looked at the paper and saw what was written on it:
Help us!
I showed this to Natalie, who looked equally as confused. "What does that mean?" she asked, as if I would know.

"This may mean that this kid isn't the danger, but rather that he is *in* the danger. Let's see if we can find out where he lives."

∎∎

After asking numerous people, we found ourselves at an old shack in the nearby woods. It was rather run-down; looking more like it should be torn down instead of having someone living here. There was a medium sized fire going, but no other signs of anyone around.

"Do you think he's even here?" Natalie asked. I was about to reply when I heard a very faint whistling. In a fraction of a second, I was turned around, holding an arrow between my pinky and ring finger.

"Nice catch," I heard come from one of the trees. "Let's see you do that again. I want to apologize for sound absolutely stupid with my earlier remark, I decided to shoot arrows at you instead. Great trade off right? But, we don't want any mistakes so…" That said, Natalie rose into the air. I almost called out for her when the same voice yelled, "Fire!" For the next few minutes, I was dancing all over the place, dodging and catching any and every arrow that headed my way.

After ninety-six arrows were fired, Natalie and the boy descended from the trees. "You're good, my friend. Where did you learn to do that?"

"I picked it up along the way. But never mind that, what is so amusing about firing arrows at someone?"

"I don't get a lot of time to train my archer militia with shooting at something as large as you, Victor."
"Wait, how did you…"

"You have every right to be confused. The fact is that, I have prophecies when I fall asleep occasionally. I dreamt that one day I would meet you two. But you still don't know me. My name is Vincent Cooper."

"Nice to meet you, I think," Natalie squeaked, still shocked from her experience. "How did you lift me up?"

"I drew a picture of a wind carrying you upwards. Simple really."

"So, did you actually draw this entire town?"

Vincent groaned loudly as he heard the question. "That story again? No, this town is at least six hundred years old. I, on the other hand, am only fourteen. The young boy from the legend is one of my ancestors, though. I think there may be some truth to the myth, but how the tale could carry on today is beyond me."

"So, you have the power to create anything you draw?" Natalie asked, obviously astounded that something like this could even exist. But I did, so why couldn't he?

"Yes my friend, I do."

"So the real question isn't really 'Are you the boy of the myth,' but rather 'why you are being *called* the boy from the legend?'" I said, listening closely to everything he said. "Someone must be trying to manipulate the townsfolk to believe the myth so that they can do something."

"The only thing that could be of any value from the story would have to be the iron guardian, but I don't think that it is actually possible for someone in my family to actually make something that is A) that big, and B) is alive at the same time."

"How much of the myth do you know?" Natalie asked intent on learning as much as possible.

"You already know up to where the village was drawn up, but there is a lot more to the story than most know. After the village was big enough, the boy, Esau Cooper, hid the iron guardian under the village. He knew that, when it was needed again, he need only shout out its name and it will arise to assist.

"Many years passed, and the location and the name of the guardian were lost to everyone. The town became dependent on The Artist, which is the title given to people with my talent. But, in recent years, The Artist became shunned, forced to leave the town, being dubbed too dangerous for those who lived in the village. Five years ago, my parents, my mother being The Artist, died while helping others in the village out of a fire that had spontaneously started. And, before you ask, the power of the Artist has traveled through several family names before returning to my own. The name goes to the first-born of the family."

"Was the cause of the fire discovered?" I asked, knowing that the fire may be a key fact to solving this mystery.

"Yes, but at the same time, no. Everyone looked for a cause, but in the end, it was our police chief, Robert Puzzle, who solved it by stating that it was nothing but a gas leak that got out of hand. But I knew that my parents could have easily survived something like that. Plus, there have been more fires, once a month. All have been dismissed as gas leaks or something similar."

Something wasn't adding up. First off, Vincent had the ability to foresee the future occasionally, yet was unable to prevent his parents from dying in the fire, which should be major enough to have caused his ability to spark. But that wasn't important as of now. Second, why does this make it seem that the fires were no accident? Third, how does Mr. Puzzle tie into all of this? And finally, what connection is there between the guardian and the current day town? Then, something hit me.

"Where did the first fires happen?"

"The center of town, why?"

"And how did the town expand?"

"It expanded from the center outwards. Why are you asking?"

"One more question: Have any of the old houses ever been rebuilt?"

"No, they have been kept as monuments."

"I think I want to have a quick look at one of these monuments. This may help me solve this puzzle."

Chapter IV

We stayed with Vincent for the day, hiding in the woods, swapping stories, and hunting. We learned for a fact that as long as Vincent could draw something, he could make it appear. His ability was outstanding. If we could get him to travel with us, we would never run out of provisions. He also learned that I was a great hunting aid.

We also learned that by his "archer militia," he meant a group of statues that shoot arrows with no need of assistance. These were nothing like the Iron Guardian from the legend, but they were still rather impressive.

That was our day basically. But that night, things got really strange. Vincent took us to where he said the next fire was likely to happen. It was a rather old looking, Victorian style house. It had only one story, but from the outside it looked rather spacious. The one thing that got me thinking was the fact that, given its estimated age and the fact that these houses were never repaired, there was absolutely no possible way it could have a gas leak.

On entry, we discovered that it was not only a house. It was an old, one-room school house. And an eccentric one at that. It had an extinguished wood burning stove, rows of seats, a small desk at the front, and a few windows on the sides. Nowhere did it look like that there could be a spontaneous cause for a fire.

We looked around the room to find anything that could possibly start a quick fire. We found nothing until Natalie whispered, "Over here."

Running over to her, we found a small puddle of liquid with a string sitting in it. A short distance away from it, we found a big red container. One that would typically be used to carry gasoline. At the bottom, there was a slight crack. I smiled as I made what would become a fatal connection. *A gas leak.* It was almost comical at how obvious the whole thing was.

We followed the string all around the room, finding the end stuck in the stove. We tried to open the door, but to no avail. In the end, Vincent drew up a screen that we could use to look into it. It was filled to the brim with what looked like the same liquid we found on the floor.

"This is not a gas leak," Natalie said, "this is someone trying to destroy the building to get under it."

I got on the ground to get a better look at the liquid on the ground. I knew that this must be the key ingredient in the fires. I put my nose over the puddle and took in a small breath. I instantly dropped Face-first into the puddle. There is one thing that is for sure, I'm not immune to all liquids.

∎∎∎

I woke up a short time after, watching the school house burn down into ashes. Natalie and Vincent were staring at me with worry. They had seen my faint and had pulled me out of the building.

"What was that liquid?" Vincent asked me after I had come back to my senses. After seeing me faint, I guess neither one of them wanted to try the same stunt.

I looked up at them, smiled, and said, "In a way, there was a gas leak."

"What?"

"That liquid on the ground was gasoline. Someone must have been trying to burn the house down in an attempt to get under it for some reason."

Immediately, a group of police officers ran towards us, gagged us, and dragged us towards their cars. Natalie looked over to me and squeaked, "What's going on?"

"I think we are under arrest for blowing up that house."

"Let go of me! I know my rights!"

One officer threw a gag over her mouth as two others did the same. "Then, you should know that you have the right to remain silent."

■■■

We arrived at the jail house in no time. Before any of us could retaliate, we were thrown into a jail cell. They had confiscated everything from us that could aide in an escape then locked us up. Natalie looked like she was having a panic attack. Vincent had also curled into a ball. I, on the other hand, sat there and laughed.

"I fail to see what you find so funny," Vincent hissed at me.

"You guys don't get it? This confirms my suspicions."

"What suspicions? That the police were going to throw us in a jail cell? I knew people wanted me behind bars, but I never thought it would actually happen."

"No, that was a given. I mean that now I know who is behind this."

"How could us having been thrown in jail possibly tell you who is behind the fires?" Natalie asked. Neither one had caught what I had found out. It was so painfully obvious.

"First off, who had solved the cases?"

"Robert Puzzle."

"Correct, and how did he dismiss the fires?"

"He lied and said that there was a gas leak."

"No, he told the truth about the gas leak. However, he didn't specify what leaked, so everyone immediately assumed that he meant in the houses' pipe system. No one would believe that there was a leak in a gas can."

"So the phrase 'gas leak' was enough of a stretch to throw people off."

"Exactly, and the thing that finally got me to believe that Puzzle is behind this is the fact that we're currently in a jail cell. Him being the head of the police, he would naturally throw us in. It's the old scapegoat technique. One preforms a crime, another gets blamed do to the first's power."

"So we were just in the wrong place at the wrong time?"

"Actually, it was the *police* who were in the *right* place at the *right* time. If they hadn't already known where the fire was going to be, they would have been right there as soon as it started. But enough about that. Are you guys ready to leave?" I smiled as my hand turned back into the claw.

■■■

In no time at all, we were back at Vincent's hut. We were out of breath from both running from the jail and laughing at our escape. We even took the time to get our stuff back before we left. That one would keep people scratching their heads for years. Now for the hard part: We had to get back *into* town *without* getting caught by the police.

"I've got an idea," Vincent said, turning towards the trees. "Archers, to me!" he yelled to the statue archers. They all came out of the trees onto the ground. They came primed with a quiver of twenty arrows. Their bows were made of what appeared to be a living tree. In fact, they all looked like they were made of trees.

I smiled at the statues, knowing exactly his plan for getting us back into town.

■■■

The next morning, we prepared for our entry. Natalie and I watched as Vincent gave a quick pep talk to his 'men' on their mission.

"You were made for a time when this town needed soldiers. Now is the time. You are the protectors of this village. The normal police force has lost their purpose, so we need you to draw them out of the town while we confront their leader. Are you ready?"

"Yes!" the statues yelled out. This gave me a bit of a start, but it made sense that they should be able to talk, since Vincent had made them that way.

"Solders move out!"

Chapter V

Outside the police office, there were two officers patrolling the area. I walked towards the doors to walking into the office. Suddenly, one of the officers ran in front of us. "Halt! What business do you have here?"

"We wish to talk to Mr. Puzzle, my kind sir."

"The chief has no business with commoners like you."

I held out my hand and watched it transform into a claw. "As you can see," I said with a smirk, "we are anything but common."

Before he could protest, I picked him up and threw him through the door. As people on the other side of the door turned to look at us, I smiled and said, "Tell chief Puzzle that he has some guests."

• •

In no time, we were in the chief's office. Robert was a middle sized man, had white hair, and spoke in a gruff voice. He hadn't said more than two words when I recognized him as the man who talked to us earlier. But that was set aside for the present.

"So, Mr. Puzzle, I understand that you closed the case of the fire that broke out in town five years ago," I questioned him. Natalie and Vincent stood by the door while questioned him.

"Of course. It was really simple to figure out. Once the fire had been put out, I had my men go in and investigate. Sure enough, they found a broken gas pipe, which had caused the fire."

"But from what I understand, the fire started spontaneously. A simple gas leak is only deadly when there is an open flame. However, the fire started in one of the older buildings."

"Yes, it did. But what does that have to do with anything?"

"Vincent, maybe you can tell us why that sounds strange."

Vincent nodded. "The houses at the center of town are kept as monuments to when this village was started. Naturally, none of these houses would have gas or electricity in them. And we would never allow an open flame."

"This would mean that there had to be a different cause. Perhaps, a more explosive cause."

"What are you implying?" Robert asked with a scared look on his face. The exact look I was looking for.

"I'm saying that, since there is no accidental cause, there must have been something to cause it purposely. In this case, some gasoline being lit in search for a mythical entity: the Iron Guardian."

"What?" I heard him say in terror.

"Really, it's just a matter of putting two and two together. You here have been searching for the guardian for a while, just how long is unknown to me. Anyway, you had been using settle methods to breaking the ground to get under the city, you know, shovels, drills, etc. But you just weren't reaching down far enough. So, you decided to try your hand at explosives, causing the fire at several of the old houses. You blamed the accident on a gas leak and therefore escaped criminal judgment. And that is what really happened. Fess up, Robert."

At first, I was met with silence. The chief looked shocked at what I deduced from what seemingly little clues I had. After a while, Chief Puzzle dropped his head. "It's true. I was in search of the Iron Guardian. But I had good reason. I'm an old man and I can't continue to keep this village safe for much longer.

"You see, I've been chief of the police force of about ninety years now. Yes, you heard right, ninety years. I don't have much left in me. I'm often reminded of that by how my back breaks so easily nowadays. But one day," he pointed at Vincent, "I saw that young man's powers and was reminded about the myth of the Iron Guardian. I thought that if I could discover its hiding place, I could soon rest in peace, knowing that it would keep the town safe."

I looked to see if Natalie and Vincent were buying this. I wasn't surprised to see Natalie crying and Vincent on the verge of tears himself. I turned back to Robert and asked, "Do you realize that by burning down houses in the village, that you are doing the exact opposite of your job?"

"I realize that now. Thank you for reminding me of that. Now, I must apologize to the villagers and resign from my post." I helped him up out of his chair and walked him out of the office. Upon exit, a police officer ran up to us with a frantic look in his eyes.

"Chief Puzzle, there was a sudden break-out of statue solders from the woods and now, they are currently digging up the dirt under the remains of the old town hall."

● ●

After helping Robert into a police car, we were over at the scene. The statues had already dug a large hole in the remains. No, it wasn't a hole. It was a tunnel. Vincent drew a stairway leading into it and we helped Robert down. The tunnel looked almost as old as the village itself.

Walking down it, the tunnel opened up into a large area. It was filled with trees and a lake, amongst other things. In the center of a lake was an island, connected to the rest of the land by a rope bridge, was a large marble plaque that read:
The village of Hope is carefully guarded,
But the Guardian herself is in the hearts of the village.

"Hope, our fair village," Robert whispered. So now you know the name of the village, Hope. But what does this mean *The Guardian herself is in the hearts of the village*? I tried to make sense of it all when Natalie stepped forwards up to the plaque.

"I know the Guardian's name," she said. She placed her hands and whispered something to the plaque. Suddenly, the ground started to shake. The plaque's top opened up and a statue rose up from it. It was a large statue of a woman, who looked like a caring mother. She was made entirely out of iron, but nether-the-less, her garments flowed in the slight breeze like they were real. She looked at us and smiled, saying, "My name is Hope, but you may know me as the Iron Guardian."

Chapter VI

Vincent broke down completely, tears streaming down his face. Hope, using some kind of power she was given, shrank down to the size of a normal human. She then walked over to Vincent and embraced him. "I know you may be surprised at me, but there is no reason for you to cry, child."

"It's not that," he said, trying to smile. "It's the fact that, you look like my mother. Esau somehow knew that his descendant would need reassurance, and made you like you are." He then wrapped his arms around the statue. "You feel warm, but not like iron."

Hope smiled at the Artist. "Young member of the Cooper family, you know very little about your heritage. I'm only iron when I need to be. Right now, I have no reason to be cold and harsh like my origin. You need comfort, comfort that I am willing to give."

Natalie and I walked over to the two and helped them up. I noticed that Vincent was right. For an iron statue, Hope felt a lot like a normal human, both in weight and touch.

Just as they were stood up, Robert fell down. We ran over to the man, who was struggling to breath. He forced a smile at us. Then he grabbed my hand, bringing me to my knees. He then pulled my ear towards his mouth. He then whispered to me with his last breath, "Thank...you." His hand then went limp, no pulse went through him.

I felt tears falling down my face onto the dead man's. I then put my head to his chest, crying softly, but enough to bring Hope to my side and help me up. She then lifted him up and took him over to the lake. She set his body on the surface, the flowing water taking him a little way from the bank we sat on. He then sunk to the depths of the lake.

Hope turned to us and said, "He will sleep among the honored. Now, let us go back to the surface."

But I didn't move. How could I? That man, that very old, kind-hearted man, had died in front of me.

We came back to the surface to the awe of several villagers. There were several questions such as "What is that?" and "Where's Chief Puzzle?" and so on. Hope was a major subject of a majority of the questions.

So, to get it out of the way, Vincent drew up a small but high platform and announced, "People of Hope, I want to introduce you to the matron of the village, the legend behind the Esau Cooper. This is the Iron Guardian, but her real name is Hope. She is the one who helped to form this town. And now, along with her, I take my duty as The Artist of Hope, as my ancestors were before me."

A cry from someone in the crowd reached our ears. "What happened to Chief Puzzle?"

"This may be a shock to you all, but Mr. Robert Puzzle died while we were in Hope's Garden. But don't mourn for him, people of Hope. Hope has honored him amongst others of Esau's time. Robert was a good man, but as we all know, he was really old, roughly one hundred twenty-five years old. He never let anyone or anything stand in his way when he was after something. Let us remember this day in honor of the man who had searched for Hope, both on the inside and out."

The crowd cheered as Vincent finished his speech. He got off his platform, and with the wave of his eraser, he made it vanish. He ran over to us, smiling. "Thank you, all three of you. Without any of you, I wouldn't have been able to find either Hope. But now, I think I have."

I reached my hand out to him. "It was nice meeting you guys, but now, we need to go."

"Why?"

"Let's just say, I have someone looking for me. The discovery of Hope will definitely attract some unwanted attention."

"Well, if that's how it is, then that's how it is. But first," he drew up bag small rings. "Whenever you meet someone who you think you'll need again, give them a ring and they will come when they are called."

We thanked him and then left the village of Hope, pleased with how things turned out.

Natalie turned to me as we walked down the road, still waving back to the people of Hope. "Do you think we may even come back here?"

"Perhaps one day. But we can't stay here. If my prediction holds true, then something worse than Howlers is coming."

■■■

Natalie and I stopped for the night in a cave that was about five miles from Hope. Once inside, we made a small fire and ate some of the food given to us by Vincent. I don't know about you, but a lunch meat sandwich and water never taste as good as they do when you are on the run.

After our meal, I turned to Natalie and asked, "Do you remember anything yet?"

"I remember that... I was running from something. There were several of them, but I don't remember what."

The next thing I did felt really weird. You know that people give others rings as a sign of affection, correct? I thought I would give one of the rings to Natalie. She and I blushed as I gave it to her. "That's just in case we ever get separated," I said, my face telling a completely a different story.

"Thank you very much, Victor." She placed it on her ring finger, not helping my blushing problem any. But what really got me over the edge was the kiss on the cheek I received because of it. She really was a kind girl, and I didn't want anything to happen to her.

Now I know that I am not heartless. A heartless person wouldn't give a girl a ring. A heartless person wouldn't help an outcast solve a village old mystery. A heartless person would only feel anger and hatred. I however am kind and compassionate. I help those who I believe deserve it. However, my anger knows no bounds when it is sparked.

That night, we didn't sleep on different sides of the fire. Natalie fell asleep in my arms. I held her tightly, ready to spring into action if need be. That night was one of the only times I felt completely at rest. Her blonde hair was floating in the breeze coming from the back of the cave. We slept peacefully through the night, not at all prepared for what was going to happen the next morning.

Chapter VII

It happened early in the morning, when the world is mostly still asleep. I heard a soft cry come from the woods outside the cave. I gently placed Natalie on the ground beside me and quietly set out to investigate the sound. What I found would be the thing that would become the second most important thing in my li... existence.

I had found a baby girl, wrapped in a blanket and soft clothes, softly crying in a way that didn't show that she was upset, but just wanted to be held. But the strange part about her wasn't the fact that she was in the middle of a forest, but that was strange also. No, the strange part was what was protecting her. It was a pure white wolf, which looked both majestic and fearless. On his back was a golden cross, the vertical line going from the tip of his nose to the tip of his tail, the horizontal one across his shoulder blades.

I approached the two and the wolf looked at me, not howling or threatening to bite me. I picked the girl and started to head back to the cave, the wolf following me the entire time. It seemed that the wolf had grown fond of this little girl, and had devoted himself to protect her.

When I entered the cave, Natalie gasped at the little girl. I gave her over so she could hold her, staring with loving eyes at the child. "Where did you find her?"

"She was just a little ways out from the cave. Her protector followed us back here." I scratched the wolf behind the ears, making him nip playfully at my hand. I noticed a chain around the wolf's neck, with a nameplate that said "Guard."

"What's this," Natalie asked, finding a similar necklace on the child. "Alestina?"

"That is the name of the child, as mine is guard." Natalie and I stared awestruck at the wolf. He then spoke again. "What, did you think I wasn't capable of speech? Just because I'm a wolf doesn't mean I'm not vocal."

"Wow," I said, shocked that I was in the presence of a talking mammal of a different species. I turned to Natalie. "You heard that too right? It wasn't just me?"

"It wasn't just you." Alestina laughed as the two of us exchanged glances with ourselves and the wolf. Looking back on it, I could tell what she was laughing at. We must have looked ridiculous in our shock. "Can you talk also?"

"Oh, please. Everyone knows that young children can't speak. Coming back to reality, I ask you if we may stay with you. I cannot support this special little child much longer," the wolf said. His voice sounded like that of someone who hasn't spoken in years, which very well might have been the case. I mean, wolves don't just talk to anyone. Well, unless you happen to be a very special person yourself.

"Of course you can," Natalie said, glancing quickly at me. "But you must do one thing for us. We're leaving now and we can't carry her the entire way to... wherever we are going. So, would you please be so kind as to let her ride on your back?"

"I promise you, she will not fall off. I have carried her many miles on my back, and the whole time, she has arrived unharmed," the wolf assured us.

Natalie placed the toddler on his back, the girl cooing "Mama" as she did so. Natalie smiled and kissed her on her forehead. I could tell that she was already attached to the little girl. When the cave was cleaned up, we set off from the site, the road before us taking us who knows where.

■■

After a few days of walking, hunting, and camping, we came to a big city in Minnesota. Don't ask how we ended up there, we just headed in a random direction, flipping a coin at a few of the T-roads.

It was filled with people from all over the place, but for some reason, there was a white line down the center of the city. The people never crossed this line, but whenever interaction happened, it was like this: A person on both sides of the street would face each other, frowning heavily at each other. When trade needed done, each person would throw full forcedly what they needed to trade.

We walked down the center of the city, trying very hard to not step on either side of the line for too long, when I saw someone running towards us. He was wearing ragged clothing that suited someone that lived in a hut rather than a city-dweller. Running after him was a man wearing something that should belong in a museum's rarest and most expensive clothing section.

When the raggedy man crossed the line, the wealthy one stopped and turned away, happy with what he accomplished. That's when I noticed what the line was for. It separated the wealthy people from the poor ones. The buildings were built in such a way that no matter what time of day it was, not even the shadows would cross the line. We continued walking down the line until I slipped and fell down a hole, discovering an underground slide. I would have enjoyed the ride a little more if it hadn't snuck up on me like that.

At the bottom of the slide, I dodged Natalie and Guard then had to catch Alestina. The little girl was screeching with laughter from the ride. Just as we regained our composure, a young man and woman ran into the room. The girl looked like she belonged to the wealthy side, while the boy was from the other side.

"Oh my goodness! Are you alright?" the girl asked. The couple ran up to us and helped us get up. "I'm so sorry about that. We really need to hide that tunnel better."

"Believe me," I said, "It was hidden really well. Natalie, are you alright?"

"Yes, I'm fine. How about you and Alestina?"

"Oh we're just peachy, aren't we gorgeous?" I asked the toddler, tickling her stomach a little, making her laugh her sweet little laugh. This must be what a father feels like when he's really close to his daughter. It makes you feel warm on the inside. It makes you feel like you'd do anything for your children. I wonder what having a father felt like.

"Follow us and we'll get you settled a little. By the way, my name is Martha Crates. And this is my boyfriend, Jason Everlasting."

"It's a pleasure to meet your small family," Jason said, bowing slightly.

"Oh, were not married."

"But isn't that your child?"

"Well, yes... but no. We found her in the woods a few days ago. And we're taking care of her until... can we get off this topic please?" Natalie asked, her face now really bright red.

"Of course," Martha said, bumping Jason slightly. The rag-clothed man just smirked at her.

■■

Eventually, we were in a simple family room. It had two couches, a large chair, and a small fire place. Right now, Martha and Jason were telling their stories to us.

"As you may have guessed, this civilization is broken up into two groups, the rich and the poor basically. They have actual names, but this a young child in the room. My father is the mayor of the wealthy side, while Jason's is the leader of the poor side. We were always taught to hate the other side of the line. So that's how our lives went until the day I turned seventeen. We both got into an argument that is now way too pointless to bring back up when we fell down one of the tunnels.

Jason took over from here. "When we reached the bottom, we landed in a way where she fell on top of my chest. We gazed into each other's eyes for a while and forgot all our differences. Down here, we discovered what appeared to be an underground house, the one that we're currently sitting in now, that was too nice for me yet too cheap for her. Its proof that once, money didn't matter the most to other people. We've been together since."

I was amazed by their story. The poor boy and the wealthy girl, the couple of misfits. After a while, I said, "Well, we can't keep you two separated by a financial barrier now, can we?"

"What can you do?" Martha asked with hopeful eyes.

"I want honesty from around the room. How many of you have heard the word 'hostage?'"

Chapter VIII

The next day, we had everything set up. My plan went like this: I was going to take Martha "hostage" and threaten to drop her if I didn't receive the outrageous sum of five billion dollars, more money than was in the city at any given time, by midday. However, when Martha's father fails to pay the price, Jason is going to come up and "fight" me for Martha. The result is going to be me falling to my "death," slipping down one of the several tunnels that we decided on earlier.

We were at the part when I was dangling Martha over the side of a building. She was screaming her heart out, though I couldn't tell whether it was because she was acting or out of genuine fear. A crowd was gathering, still on their designated sides of the line, there all the same. Martha had just called out for her father when I jumped into action. "Whose daughter is this?" I called to the crowd below.

"She is mine, you greedy little..."

"If you want me to be greedy, then I'll be greedy. Let's make a trade for this little girl then. Three billion dollars for the young girl's life." This was going almost too perfectly. "Pay me by midday, or say good-bye to Ms. Crafts."

"It's Crates! Short a! Long e!" Martha screamed. Now I think she was screaming out of fear. I wanted to reassure her, but that could jeopardize the whole thing. From the crowd, I saw Jason start running up the stairs. I was on a reasonably tall building, so I hoped I didn't have to wait until midday.

Once he got to the top, though, things got out of hand. I heard a jet appear from overhead. It had the Special Team's insignia on the side so I knew exactly who it was, but the question was, how did they possibly find me? I had little time to act so I quickly thought of the one thing that could possibly end this so everyone wins.

I had Jason throw me over a little early so he could save Martha. Notice the word "save" wasn't in quotes that time? That's because they were really in danger now. I drew the ship away by falling into the tunnel. No one would look for my body, so everyone would naturally think I'm dead.

■■

I stayed in the underground house for the rest of the day, waiting for the others to come and find me. When they did, I couldn't believe the looks on the faces of Martha and Jason. Apparently, the plan failed. Martha was brought back to her father, but Jason was chased away because he had touched her "perfect silk dress."

"You know what? That's it! I know exactly how I'm going to solve this problem!"

"How do you propose to do that, pray tell?" Martha asked with tears in her eyes.

"I'm either going to have them come to their senses or kill them!"

"You wouldn't do that."

I felt my hand boil as it changed. This time, it wasn't a claw. It was a scythe. The tool that was usually used for harvest. I held up my hand to show all in the room, except Alestina, because she was asleep in a bed in next room. Guard walked up to me and nudged me with his head.

"Settle down, Victor. There must be a better way for this to work."

"Then tell me. Tell me, Guard, how I could possibly make this work."

Natalie put her hand on my shoulder. "Please calm down Victor. I know you wish this had worked, but it didn't. But no one has to die to get your point across." I looked her in the eye. Those two, piercing golden eyes that could stare into your very soul were looking at me. They were pleading with me. And I was powerless against them.

I felt my hand change back. I was not a monster. "Alright," I said, in a humbled tone, "you guys win. How do you propose to erase the line in the middle of your fair city?"

"We plan to go with you, hand in hand, walking out of the city," Martha said. I had to admit that it was as good a plan as any. I still liked my plan better though.

So that's what we did. The next day, we walked out of the city. Martha and Jason, walking out of the city, each wearing the golden ring I had given them, hands intertwined with each other. Some people were happy about the two. Most were disgusted that they would even think about walking together, let alone hold hands. And I knew that all of them were surprised that I was still alive.

There was a slight silence, as if they were honoring the moment. I hadn't even been awake very long and now, I have changed the lives of those in two settlements. Maybe that was my destiny, to change the lives of those who need assurance. My face almost betrayed my inner feelings with a smile, but I quickly stiffened my face so that the frown would stay.

■■

Before long, we had left the city far behind. The older couple was overjoyed. "Thank you," Martha said as she tightly gripped Jason's hand. They stared into each other's eyes, thinking they knew that everything was going to be alright. I didn't have the heart to tell them that they couldn't be more wrong.

We were in an abandoned shed in yet another wood now. It looked like it may have once served some kind of storage purpose, but now it was to be our temporary home. Natalie and Martha kept a close eye on Alestina while Jason, Guard, and I went hunting for something that night. We had just gotten out of ear shot when Jason asked me something.

"So Victor, what are you? I know that you are not human, but you could blend right into a crowd unnoticed until someone got you angry."

"I'm the most deadly weapon that can be found on this planet as of now. I couldn't be more dangerous unless..." I was cut short be a gun going off towards me. The bullet stopped dead in the air, but I knew that the other two weren't safe. "Get back to the girls!" I yelled to them, facing my attackers.

Yet again, the special team has found where I am. They were in an enclosing circle around me, each one firing bullets at me. I felt my hands claw up as I turned to face them all. They had no idea what I was capable now. The shower of bullets rained down on me as I whispered into the air, "Vincent Cooper." I felt a change in the air slightly, and then next to me, within my "force-field," Vincent popped out of the air.

"Are you ready to party?" I asked. Vincent just smiled as he started drawing up something. I was staring the special team down when I heard a loud growling sound. That drew all of our attention to the creature behind Vincent.

It was a large beast, covered in yellow, shaggy fur. Its mouth was filled with four rows of razor-sharp teeth. The tail flicked back and forth behind it, slicing anything in its way cleanly. On its shoulders were two mounds, covered in spikes, dripping some green liquid. It lifted its head up and let out a blood-curdling roar, releasing a turret of fire as it did. It lashed out at the Special Team, focusing on a hit and run technique.

The rain of bullets turned toward the creature, the bits of metal bouncing off its hair. It growled again, silencing the guns from ever trying to fire again. It sprayed the green liquid at us, only missing Vincent and me because of the shield around us. It turned out that it caused paralysis to whatever it touched. The Team hit the ground like rocks.

The beast then turned towards us and bowed. Vincent ran over to it and got on its back. They vanished from the area, leaving me with the fallen men and woman. I stood over Peter staring closely at his open eyes. The eye color now assured me that I had no clue what was going on. His eyes were the exact same color as mine and Natalie: gold. I ran off from there, a tear starting to form in my eye.

Chapter IX

I woke up the next morning in a strange field, covered in golden daisies, as far as the eye could see. The scene was beautiful, but I didn't know why. Maybe it was just the peaceful atmosphere around the place that intrigued me. Or maybe, just maybe, I felt that because I remembered it from somewhere.

Taking in the scene, I saw a man with royal blue robes and a gem-covered crown. He was looking at me with a smile on his face. He spoke in a kind tone, like that of a grandfather talking to his grandchildren. "Greetings, Victor. I've been waiting to speak with you for a long time now.."

"Who are you?"

"My name is of no importance, but you may refer to me as the Dream Lord. I have the ability to talk to others via dream, as my name implies. I've taken great interest in your own abilities."

"My abilities?"

"Abilities, skills, trade, take your pick."

"What is there to take interest in? I exist to cease the existence of other things. My abilities are no more than weapons at the disposal of my masters."

"You still haven't figured it out? You may have been created for one intended purpose, but I can see you have a greater destiny. But in the end, it all comes down to what you choose. Take this field for an example. If you continue to follow the path you choose personally, this could be the equivalent of the outcome. Remember, they wish to use you as a puppet. They can't do that if you don't let them. "

"What makes you so sure that I will choose the right path?" I attempted to bring out my claws, but something was blocking them.

The Dream Lord smiled at my attempts. "Those don't work in my domain. And to answer your question, I know what lies within your heart. I know that you will choose your predestined path."

"And if I don't and follow the path that my creators have set for me?" Suddenly, the field began to catch fire. All around me the flames were rising. It seemed that they were coming from even the sky. Looking up, I saw a horrible beast, with giant claws, gnashing teeth... and gold eyes.

■■

I sat bolt upright when I awoke. That may have been a dream, but it felt way too real. It was still dark out, which must mean that it was only a short time after I had dealt with the Specials and moved us to a different place to set up camp. Our fire was still cackling from the logs we had put on it.

Martha, Jason, and Guard were all asleep. Natalie, however, was up, looking at me with worry as she cradled Alestina in her arms. "Victor, are you alright?"

"Y-Yeah I'm fine. I just had a bad dream. Did I wake you up?"

"Little Alice beat you to it. She started to cry a little before you woke up. Are you sure you're alright? You look a little pale."

How could I tell her what I had just seen? She is my best friend, and I didn't want to trouble her with my worries. I sighed as I did a quick run-down of my existence. It was full of troubles that only someone like me could experience. I did my best to throw on a smile and turned back to the girls. "Alice, huh?"

"Yeah, I thought it was shorter than saying 'Alestina' every time we need to say her name. Besides, Alice just sounds a lot cuter." The child cooed at us as her name was called. This child, this little bundle of joy, has brought meaning into my life, and we didn't even know where she came from.

"May I hold her?" I asked, wanting the feel of her again. Natalie nodded, but as she began to hand her over, a grabbed both Alice and her in a hug. Natalie returned the embrace, and Alice started to giggle. These two special people were the most important things in my life. I kissed both of their foreheads before lying back against a tree, still holding them in my embrace.

It wasn't long before Natalie and I were the only ones awake. It felt good to have her so close to me. She turned her head to look at me with her golden eyes and smiled. "You know Victor? You would make a great father."

"And you a great mother. I'm sure that someday you will have a nice little family of your own."

"But you won't?"

"You know as well as I do that I can't be with a normal person. I'm a danger to everyone."

"Even to Jason and Martha? To Alice? To me?" She had a look of worry in her eyes.

"Natalie, I promise that, as long as I am here, no harm will come to you. I would never imagine hurting anyone without reason, especially you." I kissed her cheek softly before she said and did what would be the most important thing she could say or do.

She held out one of her hands in front of the two of us. I noticed that her skin started to bubble. Before long, a claw sat in the place of her hand. I looked in surprise at what just happened. I now knew for sure that Natalie Star was like me: a B.W.M.D. Though I expected it for a while, there was still every possibility that I could have been worng. She smiled at me before she uttered a single phrase, "I love you."

∎∎

The next morning, we headed due west. I couldn't explain it, but it felt that something, or someone, was calling me to go in that direction. The others looked confused, but Natalie finally said, "One direction is as good as another as of now. Let's go west." Not long after, we found ourselves in a small town, slightly bigger than Hope, yet smaller than the city where Jason and Martha were from. The strange thing about it wasn't its size, but its population: zero.

We made our way to the entrance to the town when we were met by an old man in a prospector's outfit, not a strange outfit for the terrain we had reached. He had shaggy gray hair all over his face, was missing a few teeth, and spoke with a voice that belonged more to a bear than a little man. "Leave, now! Leave, now!" he called to us. I thought nothing of it, given that I was likely to hear that no matter where I go. "Leave, now! The wolf master will get you!" That, however, caught my attention.

"The what?"

"The wolf master. Legend had it that this town was once bustling with people from all over. Ohio to Texas, they would come around for a chance to see some of the gems that came from that mine over there." He pointed to a nearby mine shaft in the mountains. "But then, on the night of the full moon, a man traveling with a pack of wolves came, looking for a place to stay.

"No one would provide a place for him. There were various reasons, but the main one was that they were intimidated by the wolves. Fuelled with rage, he sent his wolves on the townsfolk. The town was cleared out in an hour.

"But according to the tale, he still comes around, on the night of the full moon, searching for someone to give him a room. For you that don't know, tonight would be not only the night of the full moon, but the anniversary of that very night. Leave, now!"

We exchanged glances amongst ourselves. I wanted to ask if he was serious, but Hope was just a legend, and we still found her. Why couldn't the wolf master be real, also? To the great distress of the rest of the group, I said, "Alright, we're staying in a ghost town tonight. Anyone want to do otherwise?" Just about everyone raised their hand. "That's nice, but too bad."

Chapter X

We looked at the houses and decided that we would stay at the hotel centered in the middle of town. If this ghost was looking for a room, he would naturally go to the hotel. We made ourselves comfortable in two of the rooms, Martha and Jason taking one, Natalie, Alice, and I taking the other. Guard felt quite content on staying in the lobby of the building. "If I see anyone, I'll growl."

The rest of the day was spent sight-seeing the town. You have absolutely no idea how much we all would have given to see the town during its heyday. There were the remains of a huge fountain in the center of town, covered in dust from the years of neglect. There were several other odds and ends through town, but too many for me to list. I couldn't imagine any other reason than the myth being true to run the people from the serene town.

An hour or so before sunset, a jeep came down the road towards the hotel. The old man continued shouting at them, but he was ignored again. When the jeep came to a stop, two people came out of it. A man, that looked like he would be more at home in the Australian outback that in the American West and a woman who looked like she came from the sun-bleached state if Hawaii. Natalie and I ran down to meet them.

The man held out his hand and said, in the voice that confirmed my stereotyping, "My name is William Dagger, and this is my wife, Sheila. We were on our way to California when we saw this little town and just had to stop by and check it out."

I took his hand in my own and shook it. "My name is Victor Forte, and this is my friend, Natalie Star. We were traveling also and decided that we would stop here for the night. I suppose that you can stay here at the hotel as well. We're here only with a few friends, so there is plenty of room. May I say that it is a pleasure to meet you both?" We led them into the hotel and showed them one of the many rooms that was still open and let them get settled. "What we have, we're pleased to share," I said as we left the two in there room.

Back in the entrance, the old man was standing there, his arms crossed, his face in a frown. "I tried to warn you, but you wouldn't listen. Now don't blame me when you're being hunted down by a pack of wolves with every intention of ripping you limb from limb." He walked off into what was left of the sunset, seeming to vanish as he walked towards it.

I had no idea what to think of this. The man was already crazy; I didn't want to think about him right now. I turned from the sunset to enter the building when I heard a wolf howl. I thought it was Guard, up until I realized that he was still in the building. I sent a shiver down my spine as I thought about the myth.

Chapter XI

I sat there in the lobby with Guard that night. The rooms that were filled now had sleeping people in them all. I decided that since I had absolutely no intention of having another conference with the Dream Lord anytime soon, I would stay with Guard.

"What do you think of this wolf master story?" I asked the wolf, wanting a wolf's perspective on this whole thing.

"I guess it's possible. I mean, you seen several things that shouldn't exist, yet do. Vincent, Hope, myself. Even you, for that matter."

"I guess you're right, but still..." I was cut off by a knocking sound. Guard and I looked at each other. Then, without thinking twice, we ran to the door and threw it open.

Standing there was a man, maybe about thirty, wearing a long, black tail coat with matching top hat. Under this, he wore a white shirt, black pants, and brown boots. He held a long, ornate cane made of what looked like branches and flowers in his left hand. His voice sounded distant, like I was hearing the echo of what he said.

"My good man, I ask you kindly, do you have a spare room that I could stay in? I am a weary traveler and greatly wish for a place to rest my tired limbs."

"Y-Yes, of course. Come in, please. What we have, we're glad to share." He walked in and followed us upstairs to one of the spare rooms. We had purposely saved one of the biggest and most comfortable of them just in case someone came late at night. Specifically, if he came during the night. I was no ghost hunter, and had no intention on running into ghosts, but I could deal with people.

He turned to us and smiled. "Thank you. I won't be a burden, I assure you. Oh, and will you be so kind as to take care of my pets? We traveled a very long distance and we're all tired." Without replying, I ran down to the lobby, which now held at least twenty shadowy beasts. They appeared to quiver on the edge of existence. They snarled at us, but Guard translated for me.

"They say, 'Thank you for helping our master, now we can rest.'" All of the wolves, including Guard, howled into the night. They were obviously happy that now they could stop asking for a place.

Suddenly, the old man came in, along with William and Sheila. "There are the hounds!" They tried to grab the shadow wolves, but failed, either because one would jump out of the way or it would quiver out of reach. Everyone upstairs ran down, looking grouchy for being woken up in the middle of the night.

"What's going on here?" Martha asked. It was self-explanatory, but she still asked the question. The old man started to answer, but was instantly tackled by Guard. The shadow wolves joined the real one as the trio attempted to fend them off.

Soon, I heard screams of fear and pain as the wolves started to land some of their more painful attacks, most likely from teeth and claws. The night filled with howling from all three parties. Natalie and I were nearly floored because of the pitch Shelia was screeching at. I winced at each of the following shouts.

Soon, they were out in the streets, heading for the mine. Guard stood back as the shadow wolves ran them in. The sound then amplified, actually pulling us to the ground. The last thing I remembered was the man walking up and standing over me.

■■

I awoke in one of the beds provided by the hotel. Natalie was in my arms, sleeping like none of the events that had transpired actually happened. It was almost dawn when I heard something from the next room. Carefully sliding out from under Natalie, I got out of bed and walked into the next room.

The man was there, looking at Alice sleeping in her crib. He learned over and placed a kiss on her forehead. He turned to me and said, "This child has great potential. You must continue providing for her. One day, she will become very important. Before I leave you, I want you to know that I am no ghost. I am the being of a person with a great will. I remained here because I still have a use here."

"Are there others like you?" But he didn't answer. Instead, he lifted his hand to show a golden ring on his finger, a gesture that meant that he would come next time he is needed. When the sun finally came over the horizon, he slowly faded from sight, smiling the entire time.

Natalie came into the room just as I was picking Alice up out of her crib. She smiled, but still looked muzzy from her rude awakening. "Could you please explain what happened last night, please?"

"Let's just say that the wolf master won't trouble this town any longer." I walked over to her, wrapped an arm around her and smiled. "You, however, look like you want to have a talk with the hair master."

She responded by kissing my cheek. "You don't look much better, you know. High frequency sound weakness, huh? That's pretty cheesy." We both laughed at this comment. Someone once said it's not easy being green. Well, it a heck of a lot harder being a B.W.M.D.

We left the room to meet Jason, Martha, and Guard before we left the hotel. As we walked away, I turned to look back at it. I may have been seeing things, but I thought I saw the wolf master, smiling and waving good-bye. I raise my hand to wave back, but put it back down when the others shot me confused looks. "Just stretching," was my excuse, and the topic that was never started was dropped, just like that.

Right before leaving the town, we came upon a sign that stated the name. The name struck me as amazing and coincidental. The name: Forte Gulf.

■■

We continued westward, my intuition still screaming to go in that direction. Along the way, we met several people and solved hundreds of puzzles. Each night, the Dream Lord showed me that there was a difference between what I was and what I could be. Every dream ended similarly, some major catastrophe, followed by my image in the sky, smiling at the chaos that followed.

One night, while we were camping in a major city park, I told the others about my dreams. They all listened intently as I wove the tale of my many dreams and the message that was always stated.

"It seems to me that you're on a dangerous path," Jason said. *Thank you, Captain Obvious.* I was starting to wonder what Martha saw in him.

"Or is it that the dangerous path is the one he is straying onto?" Martha asked Jason. My question was now answered: They both have random philosophy that occasionally makes an ingot of sense.

"All I know is that I, and possibly Natalie also, are meant for absolute destruction. I mean, if someone wanted to make something as dangerous as us, they would naturally want to cause the destruction of something or someone else."

"Uh, Victor?" Natalie asked.

"And the only goal in my life is to destroy that something or someone. Then what use do I have?"

"Victor."

"I also want to know if what I have is called life, if I was grown in the prospect of destruction. Once my goal is complete, I might as well go die, if dying is even possible for something like me!"

"Victor!"

"What?" Then I saw exactly what she was calling me for. She was holding Alice in a way that her back was turned to us. Sticking out of the toddlers shoulders were two little, blue, reptilian wings. They fluttered as if she had intention to fly away. "How did those..."

Natalie let go of Alice. Instead of falling to the ground, she flapped her wings and flew around us. Guard chuckled in amusement. "Little Alestina finally got use of her wings."

I pried my gaze from the flying toddler to the talking wolf. "What the heck does that mean? What is she?"

"Alestina, now you know, is not human at all. She is a species called Morian, from the kingdom of Mora. This is just one of her several abilities, the others will come along soon now. I'm sure of it."

"Mora? As in, King Tarnek and the Morians?"

"The very same. But that doesn't matter. We should all get some more rest before..." That's all he could get in before a high pitched sound floored me.

■ ■

I awoke in a dark room with no doors or windows for me to go through. I placed a hand on the wall, but instantly drew it back from the sharp pain that followed. There were only two questions going through my head: Where am I and what material is this room made of? I tried to bring out my claw, but it disobeyed, as if it had a will of its own and wanted the day off.

Okay, I thought, *calm down and address the problem.*

The room was a seven foot by seven foot room, tall enough to allow my five foot six figure stand up straight, and wide enough for me to walk around. There were no lights in the room, but my eyes were adjusting to the dark. There was a small desk and chair for me to sit at until... until what? Why was I even here? And what happened to the rest of the group? Were they in a similar room, with no way out?

Suddenly, a voice called out to me. "Welcome to the arena! You have been chosen for a competition to the death with twenty-four other competitors. Your prize, other than your life, will be the freedom of your friends. Not to mention fame, fortune, and much else."

"What if I don't want to fight?" I asked, trying to turn the tables in my direction.

"Then you will remain here, powerless and weak. Easy enough for us to kill you faster." I opened my mouth to yell something back when one of the walls flung open. I rushed out, nearly shouting at being free, when I saw where I was.

"I'm definitely not in Kansas anymore," I said to myself. Not that I was in Kansas to begin with, mind you, I just wanted to make a reference. I took five steps forwards when a spear flew towards me. It didn't stop, so I had to normally dodge out of the way. I glared in the direction it came from.

There stood a creature that looked as far from human as possible. It stood ten feet tall, was extremely muscle-bound, and had a thick layer of fur covering its entire being. He had on his back a quiver of spears, which he reached for so he would have something else to throw at me. "Beast crush tiny human!" howled the beast. He ran at me with intense fury, raise the spear with every intention to pin me to the closest surface. I easily side-stepped him and tried to bring out my claws again, but to no avail.

Beast ran at me again. This time, I got on his back and held tight to his fur. He howled with anger as he tried to fling me of his back, making me tighten my grip on him. I climbed up his back to his neck and, when I was wrapped around it, squeezed with all my strength. He dropped first to his knees, then to his face, deprived of breath. Eventually, he had gave up and died right there, becoming my eighth victim.

Chapter XI

So, there I was, walking through what was to be a murder-fest. It reminded me very much of some other competition, but I couldn't remember what it was. Due to the fact that somehow they had implanted a weakness into me, I was now one hundred percent human, so that included the normal memory span of only remembering what I had personally gone through.

Looking back, I now find it ironic that, though I was created to cause death, I hated causing it. I'm now sure that I am not heartless. The first and foremost thing on my mind was *not* "Yay! I get to kill people." It was "I hope the others are okay."

I choose where I walked carefully, due to the fact that, thanks to Beast, I had absolutely no idea what could be in here. I took in the landscape of the arena: I was in a large forest, with a huge lake not far off. Though hilly, the land was smooth. I would almost have called it beautiful, if I hadn't known the amount of blood that had to be spilled.

I was within yards of the lake when I was flung to the right by a blast of sound. Looking in that direction, I saw my worst nightmare: an army of twelve Howlers. This was the deadliest number of Howlers that one could find outside of a war. A squadron of twelve meant this was a band of killers. Any higher number of them and you would think a war was going on. They had me at a definite disadvantage because now I was both powerless and they could screech at way too high vocals.

They were inhaling at extremely too fast a speed. As if it were a reflex, I jumped out of the way, just as they leveled forty yards behind where I was laying. That's when I saw what was keeping me weak: a little, blinking tracer in my left arm. I would worry about that later. First, I had to take care of the creatures currently trying to kill me.

They shot another blast of sound in my direction, which I again jumped out of the way of. This time, I shimmied up a nearby tree. Just as I hoped, the tree was thin enough to bend under my weight, right in the middle of the Howlers. They all turned inwards and shouted at me, each blast of sound missing me by mere millimeters. The Howlers then fell like flies, each being struck dead by another's blast of sound. I looked around, half cheering, half pitying.

Setting my feelings aside, I focused on my arm. This flashing little light was the reason I was grounded here, unable to retaliate in my normal way. I looked around and found a sharp rock. Bracing myself, I pressed it against my skin, slicing through a layer.

I dropped the stone, howling in pain and clutching at the wound. The pain was almost unbearable. Then I picked up the stone again, knowing that the sooner I got this over with, the sooner the wound would heal. I broke off a nearby tree branch, took off all of the leaves, stuffed them in my mouth, and continued cutting. Each time the rock came down in the wound, I wanted to drop it and clutch the wound, but I pressed on.

I almost got it out. Now, I could get a grip around it. I pulled, increasing the pain by fifty. With one last tug, the tracker was out. I dropped it beside me and the pain stopped. My skin instantly grew over the wound, which I took to believe that my suffering was over for the present. I took the tracker in my hand and crushed it, watching the little pieces of material float away before it could take effect again.

In my head, I did a quick head count. I smiled at the results: thirteen down, eleven to go. I stood up, brought out my claws, and walking carelessly through the woods. I was reassured that I was once again invincible. Nothing was going to stop me from ending this thing alive.

■■■

Soon, I had come across a little haven in a serene part of the woods. Now I could say that it was beautiful. There was a small pond, almost a deep puddle, surrounded by bushes that contained hundreds of edible berries. I relaxed here for the rest of the day, making some half decent defenses from the surrounding trees; I even made a pretty good bow and a quiver of fifty arrows. That night, I lay huddled in my make-shift bed, watching the starry skies.

Suddenly, a symbol of some kind of organization, with the letters P, A, N, M, and another A, flashed across the sky, as if it were projected onto a large screen. Before I could ponder what they stood for, it changed to show a list of creatures. I believed that this was the list of deaths that had occurred, when, scanning through it, I saw my own face. I was proven correct when the word "Retired" flashed over the pictures.

I smiled to myself, knowing that I had almost won this. I was considered dead, or rather "retired," which meant that no one would come looking for me. Also, the number of pictures was twenty, which meant that, including myself, there were only six of us left.

Unexpectedly, a bright light flashed through the trees. It knocked me into the pond. I wondered what that could possibly be when I heard a loud roar, a high screech, and then silence. From what I knew, nothing on Earth could possibly make that sound.

I was still pondering this when suddenly, I heard a rustling to my left. I instantly got up into a crouch, strung my bow, and waited for my attacker. He came out of the brush in front of me, blood dripping from his mouth. A reptilian creature that was the height of a short man, he sneered with his mouth full of razor-sharp teeth.

No more surprises for me. In the blink of an eye, I had my bow at the ready. I had six arrows in him before he could even reach me. The downside was that none of these seemed to faze him. Seven, eight, nine, and he was still coming on strong. Ten was almost to him when he got one of his gigantic hands around my neck.

He was actually crushing it. Here I was, dying in the same way that Beast had.

Gasping for air, I gripped the reptile's hand with my claw and squeezed with as much force as I could muster. It wasn't much, but it was enough for the creature to let go of me. In a flash, I was on the beast's back, my arms attempting to return the favor that he gave me. His neck, however, was overly protected by scales, so it didn't give in.

This amused the beast a little too much. He started to smash his back into nearby trees in an attempt to squash me. It was getting to be unbearable after a while. I brought one of my claws in line with where his heart was positioned, the right side instead of the left. He smashed against another tree, driving the claw into his back.

The beast howled into the night, enraged at the pain I had caused. For someone with this great of protection, he wasn't very smart. He continued to bash and crash into nearby trees, driving my claw deeper and deeper into his back. After about thirty minutes, though it felt closer to an hour, he was on the ground, bleeding from the hole now in his back.

Doing it more and more didn't make killing any easier, but if it had to be done, and there was no other choice, I would oblige without any argument. On the other hand, those scales were immensely tough, since it took a long time for my claws to get through them to the skin.

An hour or so later, I had myself a suit of scaly armor, complete with helmet and shield. Under normal circumstances, I would have felt horrible killing and skinning the beast. However, these were not normal conditions that I was working in. This was a fight to the death between the remaining five of us. I started heading back to the lake, where I was two campfires, one on each side of the lake.

"So it's all downhill from here," I said to myself. Of course, I wasn't talking about me, but rather the four poor souls that now sat on the sides of the lake. I walked towards the eastern fire first, right claw at the ready, shield in my left hand.

As I closed in, I couldn't believe my eyes. These two creatures, both of them men, were currently sharpening the claws on their right hands. Looking at the face of one, I saw something that spooked me: a dirty golden-brown eye color. They were B.W.M.D.'s! Well, not exactly, because of their eye color. They were more of half-blood B.W.M.D.'s. Half-blood obviously meaning that they were part human.

Before I could act, one of them rushed towards my position, jabbing at my throat. I parried with my claw, jabbing the other one into his side. This released a howl of pain and anger. He then tried to rip through my armor, bouncing off of it as I had when it was still on its owner. I slashed his face, leaving a good sized mark where I made contact. He ran towards the other one, who immediately took his place.

This second one was taller than the other, so he focused much of his energy at my head and shoulders. I have to say that he wasn't very skilled at what he did. This was proved by the fact that half of the blows he threw at me I just bounced to the side, leaving him open for me to rip his gut.

He growled in the direction of his friend, who, until then, was just sitting on a nearby rock, holding his eye as if it were going to fall out, which may have been the case. I have no idea how much power I put into the blow I gave him. He then ran to my left, the other to the right. Claws out and sharpened, they rushed at me with absolutely no intention of stopping.

Taking this as an opportunity to finish this fight, I jumped over the left one's head, causing them to run the other through with their claws.

They both hit the ground like rocks. One of them was already dead, the other held on long enough to ask me, "Who are you?"

"Your worst nightmare's nightmare." I slashed his face again, killing him finally. I looked around and saw a jackal looking man holding a sword was standing behind me. He was about to strike the two I had just killed when I did the deed for him.

He looked shocked at what I had caused, his mouth hanging open. Suddenly, he fell to the ground. I rushed over to him and checked his pulse. I smiled at what I discovered; He died of the very symptom I had diagnosed him with: shock. I then picked up the bodies, one at a time, and threw them into the lake. I was not honoring them, as Hope had to Robert. I was simply cleaning up my new campsite.

And that night was to be my last. In the arena, I mean, not in life. That night, after going through what spoils of war the half-bloods had, I had a feast of deer meat, assorted berries, and a drink of something both fizzy and smooth at the same time. The campfire provided necessary warmth and light for the night.

First, I put the deer meat on the fire to cook. I had no idea how long I was in my cell, but I know that it felt like I had been put back into my slumber. Also, I never had time to hunt during my time here because, whenever I had done away with one creature, something else wanted to play too.

After the meat turned a golden brown, I removed it and placed it on a wet rock nearby. Next, I dined on my spoils. The meat tasted amazing, though I'm not sure if I thought that was because I hadn't eaten anything yet or because it naturally tasted that way.

The berries had a bitter-sweet taste to them, and they kind of made my drowsy. I suddenly realized that these weren't meant to be eaten of free will, but to slip into someone's food and cause them to fall asleep, making it easy to come in and strike. I put these into my pocket, believing that I may have a better use for them.

Lastly was the drink. It tasted kind of like a mixture of chocolate and peppermint. Where they found this drink will remain a mystery to me, but I'm glad that I got my paws on it.

After my meal, I lay down close to the fire, staring up at the sky. One more to go before I was home free. I was about to free my friends and continue our way westwards. Actually, now it felt like the urge came from eastwards. Had the people who brought me here overshot where I was heading? If they did, it wasn't by much. The urge was stronger here than any other place we had been. I decided to bother with this after my assured victory tomorrow. At least, I thought it was assured.

Chapter XII

After a refreshing night's rest, I started towards where the other fire had once been. Now, all that was left was a smoke stack. The resident remained there, I knew that it just down to him and me. He started walking towards me. I noticed that he was a tiny guy, wearing armor that he should not have been able to wear without some sort of support. He was carrying, or rather dragging, a giant battle axe that he had no chance of lifting.

We met on the southern beach, the center point between our campsites. Suddenly, a voice rang out from the sky. "Congratulations contestants! You are the final two in the blood bath. However, we can only have one victor, so you will be taken to a new arena. Prepare for your final battle!"

Instantly, the ground beneath us shook and started to split. We both ended up on two different platforms, each rising into the air. Though we were obviously moving at extremely high speeds, there were no vibrations or wind to assure it. On the rise up, I brought out my left claw, but my right sword. I figured that, if I could summon a sword and a claw, I could summon just about any weapon or tool I could possibly need. I also checked my armor for any signs of wear. No trouble with it. I just tossed the shield over, having no further use for it.

After roughly seven thousand feet, a platform became visible. This was to become one of our last showings, and I wanted it not to be mine. After just a little farther, we were in a large arena, a cylinder with a radius of seventy and a height of thirty. I was brought to one side of the arena, my opponent to the other.

A small man ran up to me and asked, "What's your stage name?"

Thinking for a while, I finally said, "Dragon Heart." The man whispered the name into a walkie-talkie on his shoulder, and then ran off again. Looking over to my opponent, I saw an identical man running from him. He must have asked the same question.

The announcer spoke again to the thousands of cheering people in the stands. "Ladies and Gentlemen, welcome to the arena. We have here the end to the blood bath of the century. If you would look to the eastern side, you will see our fiercest competitor and reigning champion, Axe Wielder!" The crowd cheered to the tiny man that stood opposite of me. He raised a weak hand and waved to the crowd.

"And on the western side, one of the new tributes to the games. He has shown great promise in the trials of the beasts unleashed on him. He even discovered the blocker we put into his arm to weaken him and wrenched it out. He is, at this time, wearing the skin of a Reptile (pronounced rep-TEEL), the strongest skin yet discovered on this planet. Please welcome, the challenger, Dragon Heart!"

Again, the crowds cheered. I waved my hand at them, then, thinking to show them what I had been through, I pulled back my sleeve to show the still healing place where the blocker had been. It still hadn't healed completely, but it had faded quite a bit.

"Now, because we want to give our challenger a break from his experience, we are giving him thirty minutes to converse with his companions and pick a partner before we send him into what could easily become the last fight of his life." Immediately after this had been said, two men hustled me out of the arena and into a side room. There stood Natalie, Martha, Jason, Guard, and little Alice.

The first thing we did when I entered the room was get into a giant group hug, almost pulling in my two escorts, who politely shied away at the gesture. After this, I got down to business.

"I can take one person with me, though I think I may need more than that."

"What are you talking about?" Jason asked me. "This guy is a push over."

"Last night, in the arena, I saw a bright flash. I think that it might have been him."

"That's ridiculous," Martha said. "We may not have seen the events take place, but I see that this guy has almost no muscle on him at all."

"Be that as it may, I still think that I need help."

"I'll go," Natalie said, stepping forwards. She was my fellow B.W.M.D., so I couldn't think of a reason not to let her be the one to help me. Besides, if I have to figure out if we can die, I want to find out alongside her.

I nodded just as my escorts started prodding us back to the arena. When we arrived, the announcer started back up.

"Well, it looks like Dragon Heart has brought along Dragon Soul to help him in his final hours. I sure hope she has enough lady luck in her to challenge Axe-Wielder. Those of you with weak stomachs may wish to leave the arena now. Challengers, begin battle!" With that, Natalie got out her claws and the two of us prepared for the fight of our lives. We rushed towards Axe just as he started to glow. Then, a flash of light came from him, knocking both of us backwards.

When the light faded, I was awestruck at the sight I now beheld. In the place of the scrawny, little man was a huge beast. He was about ten feet high and had a stocky build to him. He hefted the battle axe above his head and howled. The armor he had been wearing now finally acted as an asset instead of a burden.

Before any of us could react, the floor we were standing on lowered. We were now held by a smaller room with walls all around us. They may have looked sturdy, but as I learned from Axe, looks can be deceiving.

Before we could react, Axe rushed at the two of us, namesake still held high. At the last second, we jumped out of the way, leaving him to smash into one of the walls. There was a heart shaking crackle, meaning that the wall could give way soon if too much pressure was given to it. He shook his head and ran in my direction, leaving me to jump away again. He put another dent into a wall.

That last jump brought me close to Natalie. I said to her, "Don't attack him. He can't turn as fast as we can, so we can probably get him to simply run off of the platform." She nodded, jumping away as Axe bull-rushed at her. This third thud knocked off the covering walls, leaving only two support pillars left to hold us onto the crowded ship.

Axe was getting up again, completely unfazed by what he had just caused. He now rushed at me, which had to be the stupidest idea ever because I was standing at the edge. This time, I jumped over him, flipping so I could see him fall over. He jammed his axe into platform. But he couldn't get a good enough grip on the platform and he fell off, plummeting back to Earth.

Natalie and I ran to each other, cheering at our accomplishment when I noticed they weren't letting us back up. I didn't get it. We won, didn't we? Didn't... we?

"It's not over yet," I said, looking back to where Axe had fallen over the side of the platform. What now rose over the side caused me to say, "Now that's just not fair!" Here was Axe, now flying on a pair of dark red wings, back onto the platform. He smirked at us as he rose higher and higher, and then smashed down into the middle of the platform, vibrating the entire area.

He raised his head in a triumphant roar, just as I saw Natalie jumping onto his back. Axe now howled in rage as he tried to shake her off of his back. I then saw one of his wings fall off, then the other come bloodily after. Axe cried in pain at this antic, now swinging his axe in her direction.

This was my chance to end this. He had his back turned in my direction, so I easily ran and jumped onto his back. This time, I ran my sword arm through his chest. More howling came after as he stumbled towards the edge. I tried to yank back my arm, but it was jammed into Axe's chest.

Just then, I felt something on my back, pulling on me. It finally got me unstuck, just in time too because Axe's body had just fallen over the edge again, this time, he had no way of coming back.

I watched my hand turn back before I turned to Natalie. I hugged her tightly, trying to forget already the danger we had just been through. She pulled back slightly and planted a kiss on my lips.

I heard the crowd cheer as we broke our embrace, blushing at what we had just done. The platform rose back into the main body of the ship. The announcer yelled as we rose, "Ladies and Gentlemen, I give you our new Grand Champions: Dragon Heart and Dragon Soul!"

The crowd cheered wildly at this last part, then started up a chant of "Dragon Heart, Dragon Soul!" The rest of our group came rushing toward us, cheering and congratulating us along with the crowd.

■■■

We were then brought into an adjoined room to claim our prize: heavy duty backpacks, which lessened the weight of whatever was put into it, filled to the "brim" with supplies and three thousand dollars each, given in a special purse that manipulated space on the inside to compensate for the spoils put on the inside. We were then escorted to a nearby city, excruciatingly close to where the urge was coming from.

As soon as we hit the ground, we were swarmed with fans. We received the cliché "Oh my gosh, you guys are awesome!" and "That was very romantic at the end" and "Can we have your autographs?" Our escorts broke up the fans pretty quick with the promise of sending Axe's big brother on them if they didn't break up. I really hoped that they were kidding. I didn't want to put up with the elder brother of the thing I just helped kill.

Chapter XIII

After we had escaped from the crowd and our escorts, I lead, almost dragging, the rest of the group to where I felt the greatest urge was coming from. It turned out to be kind of pulsing from a large building in the center of the city, with the letters P, A, M, N, A on the side. These were the same font and orange color that was displayed in the arena the night it showed the deaths. Maybe this was where the broadcasting of what had happened came from.

Anyway, we went in and were immediately assaulted with several sterilizing sprays. Then two people in lab coats bound us up, blinded us, and led us downwards into a large room. We were unbound and our blinds removed, then we met the people in charge of the assault.

They were a thin man and woman, both with the same facial features. The only difference between the two was the length of their hair; the woman's was a slight bit longer.

"I'm extremely sorry that we had to be introduced like this," said the man, oddly enough in a French accent, "but we couldn't be sure if we would get you down here or not. My name is Professor Mess, and this is my daughter Katherine."

"Pleased to meet you," she said, holding out her hand to shake ours.

"Likewise," I mocked, shaking her hand. I wasn't amused by their "charity."

"Yes, well, we have been asked by an ancient entity that is called the Dream Lord to give you a gift."

That caught my attention. "What kind of gift?"

"This can only be injected into you and the other one like you. But in order to get it into your systems, you would have to soak in a mixture of Acidic Mercury and the substance. For the most effective transfer, you would have to... how do I put this lightly? You must remove your outer garments."

I caught Natalie's eye and noticed that her face was about the color of a tomato. I believed that mine must have been the same color. Jason began to laugh. Martha started giggling. Guard and Alice were asleep in the upper room unfazed by the attack. Finally, I said, "I suppose we might as well, if the Dream Lord wants us to do this. He must have some reason."

"I agree," Natalie stated. "If Victor will do it, so will I. Besides, I want to meet this Dream Lord and give him a piece of my mind." She was obviously talking about all the times I woke up in the night, screaming. I smiled at her and took her hand.

"Okay, if you would please follow me." The professor led us to a room containing two vats of Acidic Mercury. Natalie took the left one; I took the one the right. When I was close to the entrance, I stripped down to my boxers and then entered the vat. The deadly liquid stung a little, but I quickly got used to it. After all, I had been in one of these not long ago.

After a while, I fell asleep, not on purpose, just because I was tired from my fight with Axe.

■■■

When I awoke, I was in the familiar field of golden flowers. Looking down at myself, I was garbed in a smooth, silky, white robe, tied off at the waist with a golden belt. Turning around, I saw Natalie clothed in a similar fashion, except her garment was bluish. She looked beautiful in that robe.

As I headed in her direction, I saw the familiar third entity on the plain. "I see you've come to receive your gift. I'm sorry that my assistants were a little forceful..."

"Forceful?" I asked. "Try down right pushy. What is the gift anyway?"

"You haven't noticed? Okay, if I have to tell you, I have created a bridge between both of your minds. This bridge can be blocked or opened at will, but the connection will always be there."

"Why would you do this?" Natalie asked.

"Now that you two have... shown feelings for each other, you have become an extremely dangerous force. As you know, the forces from Area 51 are already after you. But what you don't know is that a rival group is after you. This group goes by the acronym PAMNA, though no one knows what it stands for."

"So we were created to oppose this other group?" Somehow this didn't surprise me at all. I mean, I'm a B.W.M.D. I was created for the destruction of something, and now I know just what for.

"You were created out of a race of the most dangerous weapons of all time. These two organizations are at war. Yet, they've kept this war a secret for years. One organization supposedly only started to exist. What you need to do is destroy both organizations."

"Both of them? Why both of them?"

"Both believe that the destruction of the other will benefit the world. Well, I want to prove them right, by destroying them."

Something completely unrelated suddenly popped into my head. "Vincent Cooper's prophecies. You wouldn't happen to have a role in them would you?"

The old man smiled. "Yes, my child. Vincent is another special one. It turns out that there are several people on this planet that are. The only thing that stops an ordinary person from becoming extraordinary is that they don't think they can do it. How easy it would be if people would unblock their own barriers instead of creating more for others."

"Sir," Natalie said. I almost forgot she was there. "You say these things as if we could just waltz in and do them. If you haven't noticed, there is only Victor, Vincent, and me."

"Ah, but I see several more. The couple that shouldn't be. The young Morian girl. The wolf who speaks. And there is one more, but you have yet to meet her. She wishes for her name to not yet be revealed, but I'm allowed to tell you this: Enragement equals Explosive."

■■

I was about to ask another question when I felt myself being shook awake. I was now on a table, fully clothed, but my hair was still dripping with the acid. A small basin collected this. Looking around, I could see that the only other person in the room was my Natalie Star, still lightly dozing.

I got up and walked over to her, watching her shift as she got up. I hugged her gently and planted a quick kiss on her cheek. "Did you sleep well, darling?"

She giggled at this. "Better than I have in a long time. How long were we out?"

"Five days," said a voice from the outside room. I recognized it as Katherine. "I don't know what he told you, but it must have been important."

That couldn't be right. Five days? It felt like only a few minutes. But I guess this is what it's like for normal people: sleep for an hour, feels like a second. But still, five days? Had we been given the same message over and over, just so it would sink in?"

It didn't matter; we were up now. We left the room and entered the lobby of the building. There sat Martha and Jason, who were almost unrecognizable as the couple we had brought from the prejudice city. They were now wearing normal everyday clothes, the typical outfit for adults nowadays.

Alice and Guard were closer to the door, playing something. The connection between the toddler and the canine must have been very tight for them to want to spend all of their time together.

When we walked in, the four jumped up and got us into another one of our group hugs. This was becoming a thing with us now. When one of us goes through something, we give them a big hug.

Martha was the first to speak afterwards. "So, what's the word from Dreamland?"

I turned to face Natalie quickly before I responded with, "Things are about to get... exciting."

Chapter XIV

We headed away from the lab soon after that. I surely had no intention on staying in a place that I was supposed to destroy. The first place we went was a nearby Golden Corral. I thought that I would treat them to a feast with some of our award money.

The first thing I did was get a plate with a taco, mashed potatoes, spaghetti, and pizza. Never having this food before, I savored every bite. I thought jealously about normal people who got to have such great things every day and took them for granted.

There was a learning experience here though. I learned the secret effect of Mexican food on a B.W.M.D. Apparently, my creators thought it would be funny to take the phrase 'My mouth is on fire' literally. It turns out that when the spice kicks in, it causes us to temporarily breathe fire. With such a little amount, though, the effect is short lived. I only took a small bite and that caused the reaction. Natalie had just returned from getting her food when the episode ended. She had a curious look on her face as too why I was laughing at my food, up until she took a bite of her own.

Halfway through, a tall man in a black trench coat and top hat walked over to our table. He never said a word, but simply handed me a slip of paper, then walked off again. I carefully unfolded the paper and revealed the words:
You and your friends are invited to a gathering at city hall tomorrow night.
There is no financial fee; we only ask that you look presentable.
We are celebrating the life of Mr. Robert Puzzle.

I passed the paper around the table to the others. "What do you guys think?"

Jason had a confused look on his face. "Who was Robert Puzzle?"

"You could say he was a friend of mine." Well, that was almost true. The only real thing I knew about Robert was that he was the one hundred and some year old police chief in the village of Hope. I also know that his main goal in his career was to find the village's name sake and give back her position as the protector of the village. The last thing I remember was the final thing he said to me: *Thank you.* Thank you for sparing me from facing my wrong doings.

"We might see Vincent there," Natalie pointed out. That was obvious... unless she was showing me something.

"What do you mean?"

"It may have a greater purpose than what the invitation tells. There is a good chance that members from both organizations will be there, so this may be a trap."
"Good thinking. With that in mind, who still wants to go?" There were nods from all around the table. The promise of a trap seemed to spur them on, instead of turn them away. "Alright, I'll tell you what. If you guys can get some snazzy outfits, then we'll go."

■■

I might as well have asked them to get me a handful of grass. Jason and Martha ran out to get clothes as Natalie, Guard, and I worked on our new campsite. This one was in the park that city hall was part of. I thought that if they wanted us to show up, we shouldn't disappoint. They returned around the time we had to get ready to go in. We had already seen multiple people enter the building, including some of the unobservant Specials.

When we changed into our new outfits, the only recognizable one of us was Martha, since she used to wear nice things all the time. She wore a silk dress that was common for her family. Jason had a simple black tuxedo that, when worn by him, looked amazing.

Natalie, however, had received a beautiful pink dress, with frills at the back and puffed up around the sleeves. She also had red high heel shoes and a silver headpiece. All of this, added to the golden ring she kept on made her look downright stunning.

I also received my own set of dress clothes. My outfit consisted of a white dress top, matching khaki pants, black shoes, black bow tie, and a white top hat. I had received the title of irresistible from the girls.

Alice had gotten a simple blue dress and shoes. I didn't think it was necessary for her to dress up, since she was only a toddler, but Martha and Natalie insisted that she also look "presentable." Women and their sense of fashion. Everything needs to look nice.

Guard wasn't left out either, even though the chances of him going in were very slim. Martha first brought out a brush and pair of scissors that she had bought. Without warning, she had gotten Guard on the ground, brushing off any loose hair. I had to laugh at the irony of the situation: Guard lost his guard. After his brush down, he was given a golden, diamond-studded collar and a silver vest. I began to wonder where she went to get dress clothes for the wolf.

I finally built up enough courage to ask the dreaded question. "How much did this all cost?"

Martha winked at me and said, "Not a dime. I know people."

I would have questioned further if I cared, but it was time for us to go in. I held out my arm to Natalie and asked, "Shall we?"

She blushed, and then responded with, "We shall."

The building was already filled with several people. I doubted that many of them even knew Robert, but they were here all the same. Our group quickly dispersed into the crowd, trying both to blend in and to find the real reason for the gathering.

I quickly walked over to a nearby column where I saw Alpha was standing. He was wearing a uniform that looked more like it was meant for ceremonies other than his normal patroller clothes. Standing so my back was to him, I asked, "How's your assignment going?"

He responded in a similar tone. "Rather well, now that my target has appeared."

"You don't know yet, do you?"

"I can honestly tell you that the only thing I know is that Omega has left the building in search of the nearest bar. He's probably drunk right now."

"That's not quite what I meant. Do you know what your eye color is?"

"Brown, why?"

"That's not what I saw last time I saw you. I specifically saw golden eyes. And I'll tell you another thing: mine are the same color."

"What are you trying to tell me?"

"I'm saying that you and I are the same thing. I know that half of your team is alcoholic, which means that they are rarely sober during missions where they could get their hands on something. But tell me, have you ever been shot by one of your own members?"

"No."

"That's because they can't. Bullets don't work on me, so why should they work on you? The only thing I don't understand is that, back in the facility, that high pitch screech didn't drive you to the floor."

"Oh, it did. I wondered why it only did that to me, but now I know. I learned two things today, now."

"Oh, and what would that other thing be?"

"I learned that I don't need my gun to kill you."

I took that as a hint to walk away. I may not have gotten him on my team, but at least I helped him learn something about himself. I saw Natalie and walked over to her, filling her in on what I did when I reached her.

"So, he is one of us?"

"Yes, he is. I'm starting to notice that every other person that we meet may have some sort of power, whether they're like us or not."

"It does seem to be a theme with us."

She opened her mouth to say something else when the front doors burst open. There stood a figure, cloaked in a black shirt, pants, cape, and hood, holding a small device in their hand. I discovered that it was a girl when I heard her say, "Everyone against the walls. This doesn't have to end messily."

Chapter XV

My eyes grew wide at the newest member of the party. She walked amongst the guests, looking at their faces, as if she was looking for someone in particular. One guest, an old man, shouted at her. "What is the meaning of this? Who are you?"

She turned to where the voice had come from. "I mean no one any harm, but if you tick me off, I will kill you."

"And how pray tell will you do that?"

She gestured to the giant window at one side of the room. "As you can see, I have no accomplices or guns, but it appears I have no need for them. If I may draw your attention to the object in my hand, I could tell you that this is a detonator. What does it detonate? Well, let me give you a quick demo."

She clicked the button on the device. Outside, a nearby car blew up in a massive explosion. Several of the guests gasped. The young woman in the middle of the room laughed in amusement. I, however, made a connection that I didn't know if Natalie made. I couldn't tell if she did or not because she looked one hundred percent terrified, as if she had forgotten that she was immune to explosions.

I squeezed her hand and whispered into her ear, "Enragement equal Explosive."

Her eyes shot as wide as mine did when I made the connection. This maniac was supposed to be our newest member. The problem now was how much power she had. There is every possibility that she could kill us with an explosion. We aren't immune to everything.

She continued her walked through the guests, studying the faces of each one closely. Who was she looking for? She inched, ever so slowly to where I was standing. It was the first look I could get at her face.

She had two differently colored eyes: one blue, one green. Her hair was about the same color as her outfit, and about as long as Natalie's. She wore purple lipstick and always wore an expression of boredom, maybe to conceal her inner feelings. Her skin tone was a deep, sun kissed tan, most likely from days of traveling.

When she finally got to me, her eyes became the size of oranges. Then she learned over, opened her mouth, and whispered into my ear, "Victor Forte?"

"You would be correct. What do you want?"

"I was told you have a position for me."

"Perhaps, but that all depends on if you blow us all to bits or not."

She smiled at this, and then turned to the rest of the crowd. "Everyone, get on the ground, NOW!"

No one wanted to try to resist the mad woman with the explosives, so they all hit the floor like bricks. I walked over to Martha, Jason, Guard, and Alice and lead them out of the building, holding Alice's and Natalie's hand as we did so. Someone started to follow us, but our new member whipped around and pressed the button. Vladimir was thrown against the wall by the mini explosion, causing a thud on contact.

We left the building, gathered up our campsite, and ran away from there, into the nearest forest which, luckily for us, had a series of caves. Choosing the most out of the way one, we settled there, using the remains of our fire to start a new one. Once we all had caught our breath, (hey, I said that we don't get *tired*, I never said we don't get *excited*) we finally got a chance to talk to this new demo-woman.

The first thing she did was remove her hood before she spoke. Her voice was higher pitched than Martha, but that wasn't an accomplishment because Martha had a rather low voice by comparison. "My name is Lenore. As you may have noticed, I like blowing things up."

"How are you able to do that?" I asked, already knowing the answer. "I never sensed any explosives in that room."

"That's because there wasn't any. It was all because of this." She held out her little detonator for us to see. "This device is of my father's making. For it to work, the user must focus on what he or she wants to blow up. However, it doesn't work when they try to focus on too many things at once."

I stared at the little device in her hand. A simple silver pen-like object with a green button at the tip. "So, it was all this?"

Lenore nodded. "Yes, it was all this. But the story behind it is amazing."

"Why don't you tell us about it?" Guard said. Lenore didn't even flinch when she noticed it was a wolf speaking. She treated it like it was an everyday fact.

"It's a long story."

"We've got time to kill, why not use it with this?"

She sighed as she realized the wolf had a point. Guard had a habit of getting into your thoughts in a way that made it pointless to conceal them.

"All right, you win. It all started when I was about seven…"

Chapter XVI

"One day, back when the world made sense, I was walking around the farm my family owned. It wasn't huge or too small, so it fit our family of five quite well. I heard a clanging coming from my dad's workshop and thought I should investigate.

"It turned out that he was making a series of weapons. You know, swords, javelins, shields, that sort of thing. I snuck up behind him and asked 'What are you doing?'

"He turned abruptly to face me. His eyes were twitching uncontrollably, something that told me instantly that something was wrong. 'They're coming for us, for you. I can't let them have you!'

"I wanted to ask who was after me, but just then, I heard hundreds of footsteps racing up our driveway. My father jerked his head over to the door frame, and then looked at me, thrusting something in my hands. 'Lenore, my child, run. You can no longer stay here. If they find you, I may never see you again.'

"I didn't want to disobey that order, knowing that both of our lives were at stake. I threw my arms around him in a quick hug, and then took off through the nearby woods. I had a small cave that I always went to when I wanted to be alone, so I ran there, hiding from the people that wanted us dead.

"An hour or so later, I saw that our house was in flames. I didn't know if my family was still alive or not, but at the moment, I didn't care. I just wanted to stay in my cave and hope that they would not find me.

"But they found me all the same. At first I was terrified; knowing that these people, who were cloaked the same garment I'm in now, had just destroyed my home. The only thing I had left to hold on to was the little device my dad gave me.

"I didn't know what would happen, but at the moment I didn't care. I just wanted them gone. So I pressed the button, causing a huge explosion, throwing my tormentors away into the surrounding trees.

"I was shocked by the product of the little object I held. How did that happen? Was it just because I wanted them gone? But I saved those questions for a later time and went in search of the bodies.

"Coming across one, I noticed that the clothing they wore was still completely fine, even though the explosion should have scorched everything. Instantly dropping to the ground, I worked the cloth off of the body and put it on myself. It was a little big for me then, but as you can see, it fits now. The next thing I did was go check the scene of the fire.

"I almost burst out in tears when I saw my mother and two brothers on the ground near the still burning building. I prodded them, begging them to get up, but they just lay there, as if they were asleep. I noticed, however, that my father was nowhere to be found. I felt a little better, thinking that my father had somehow survived. But I now think that maybe there were more people than the five that attacked me. I've been in search of him since that day.

"Then, about two weeks ago, while I was asleep, I was confronted by an old man. He said that he could help me by sending someone to me. He then gave me a name and description: yours Victor. He told me you were capable of so much. I knew that I had to find you. I know that you can help me find my father."

■■■

I sat there, amazed at this testimony. Here sat what has to have been the world's most determined daughter. She has been looking for her father since she was seven. That showed some awesome willpower.

Natalie, crying at the story that had been, whimpered, "So, you've only come found us when you thought that we could help you find your father?"

Lenore, still in tears herself, smiled. "I came half for that reason. But the other half was the fact that you guys need my help more than you think. Don't think for a second I'm untrustworthy. Every promise I've made I have kept."

I looked around at the rest of my team. Most were still in tears, but Guard and I were perfectly emotionless. It wasn't because we didn't find the story touching, because we did. It was because we were deep in thought.

I had to ask. "So, you sent out invitations to a number of people all over. But, how did you find where we were?"

"I didn't. I labeled it for the Arena champion Dragon Heart and hoped it would reach you. If you noticed, I didn't hand you the invite." This was true, but something in this story felt wrong, but I wasn't quite sure what it was.

Until Guard put it into words for me. "So, you're saying that you drove away five of the people that attacked your family without injuring yourself?"

She smirked at him slightly. "Who said that I didn't get injured?" With that, she spun around and slowly brought down the back of the cloak. A scar ran down the length of her back. "I got that from being blown backwards also. It caught me by surprise, so I didn't know how to react so that it would cause less pain to me. This scar reminds me what I'm looking for and why."

I guess I could buy that. Though I still had doubts about this girl. Something about her didn't feel right. I didn't know what though. She was a normal thirteen year old girl with the willpower of a lion and the mind of a rhino. But at the same time, she was beautiful enough to get anyone's attention.

I thought that maybe I should asked her something about her father, so that if I found him, I would know who he was. "What does your father look like?"

Her cheery expression dropped instantly as I brought up the idea of her father. "He is now a middle aged man, with brown hair and eyes. He is about five foot three and has a tan tone to his skin. He also has a deep demanding voice."

I liked the way she said these thing as if her father were still alive. But then I fell over backwards, scrambled to get up, and then ran out of the cave. I recognized that description.

How could I forget? That was the description of the very man who created me. The same man who thought he could call me son.

That was the description of none other than Jonathan Tell, the head scientist of the B.W.M.D. project.

Chapter XVII

I couldn't believe anything that was going on here. One of the members of my team was the daughter of the man who was the leader of an organization I had to destroy. That man had every reason to want me dead, and the only thing keeping me alive is the fact that I'm not sure if I can die.

Natalie found me first. Of course she did. She would always find me, no matter where I hid. I was currently up at the top of a tree, looking down on everything that I could see. Natalie climbed up the tree and sat beside me.

"Do you remember when we first met?" she asked.

"I remember that I saved a helpless little girl that became my best friend."

"We're more than friends now, you know. Tell me what's wrong Victor."

"Did I ever tell you the story of how I escaped from the facility know as Area 51?"

She shook her head, and I told her the entire thing up to when I met her. She was in awe during the whole thing, but when it was over, she looked puzzled.

"Why did you tell me that now? Why not before?"

"Because Jonathan Tell is Lenore's father."

She clasped her hands over her mouth. Then she asked, "You're not going to tell her, are you?"

"No, I won't. I'll tell her that the possibility of finding him is zero. It's not a lie."

"But it's also not the truth. She can't be kept in the dark forever. She will find out eventually. She probably already knows."

I scanned the trees and ground near us to see if she was near enough to hear, but she was nowhere to be found. "Let's change the subject. How are you feeling?"

She looked at me with a look of confusion. "Fine, why?"

"I'm just making conversation. It's hard to find a good topic when our whole life consists of death and being hunted down."

"I suppose you're right on that."

"So, what do you think of our scenario? I think that everywhere we go, something big is going to happen and prevent us from being us."

"And what exactly do you mean be that?"

As if it would answer the question for me, I planted my lips on hers. This one was longer than our past ones, and had more meaning to it. Breaking the embrace, I said, "That's what I mean."

We were both pretty red in the face by this point. As if to add to the effect of the moment, it started snowing. I had lost track of time by now, but I guessed that it had to be around the beginning of winter.

Natalie and I were sitting shoulder to shoulder now; her head was resting in the nook of my neck. Then, out of nowhere, Lenore had appeared on a nearby tree.

"Oh, isn't this cute?" She giggled as we both shot glances at her. "I'm sorry if I'm 'wrecking the moment' for you, but we need you back at the cave. Someone has been following us."

■■■

"Who is he?" I asked gesturing to the man tied up in the corner.

"He said his name was Matt," Jason answered.

"Matt who?"

"Correct."

"What's correct? Matt who?"

"That's his name. Matt Who. Not the most original name, but a name never-the-less."

He shuffled around in his spot, as if he couldn't figure out how he was tied. This made me not at all amused when I figured out that he *wasn't* tied up. He just had a rope draped around his wrists. I could tell that this man was an idiot.

Along with his lack of brains, he wore a suit of very high-tech armor, dark maroon in color. He held in his left hand a giant club that looked as high-tech as the rest of him. This must have been some pretty good armor if he is somehow still alive.

"Matt?" I asked him, checking if he still remembered how to communicate.

"Um, yeah? My name is Matt. I know that much for sure. Oh, and I also know that this giant lollipop is disgusting!" He swung the giant club, slamming it against the ground. The impact felt as though the very force of gravity had been shifted.

Recovering from that, I said, "Keep him safe. I need to make some calls."

Martha looked from our new guest to me and then back to me again. "Keep him safe from what?"

I groaned. "Himself."

■■

Moments later, the company in the cave consisted of Matt, Guard, Alice, Martha, Jason, the Wolf Master, Vincent, Hope, Lenore, Natalie, and me. This meeting was to plan for our strike on the two opposing bases.

"First off," I started with, "I want you all to get to know each other a little better. We're all on the same team. No, scratch that. We're all in the same family, so I don't want my 'brothers and sisters' to start off on the wrong foot. We have no need for inter-family bickering."

I gave them a while to get better acquainted, though everyone knew better than to stay next to Matt. The Wolf Master tried once, but he was greatly insulted by Matt's reply: "I see dead people."

After that, I got down to business. "Alright, as you all should know by now, there are two warring organizations that are after world domination: The world renowned Area 51 and a 'new' organization called PAMNA Our duty is to destroy both of these."

Vincent spoke up now. "And how do you propose to do that?"

"That's why I called you all here. We need plans."

"Well," Matt started, "we could lure both of the leaders into a single room, loaded with weapons of every sort, where all of us would be hiding in wait for them to enter."

We all stared at him. After a long time of silence, I finally got out, "Well, that idea is almost too good of one for you, Matt."

"And then we throw them a big surprise party!" Everyone in the cave groaned at what had once been a brilliant idea.

"As long as the surprise party consists of one of us walking up to them both, shooting them both in the face, and then walking away in *slow* motion," Jason mocked, stretching the word "slow" as far as he could without it losing emphases.

"Surprise!" I decided not to take Matt's opinion from here on out.

Hope put her say in. "How does this sound? We lure them into a large fray in the middle of nowhere. From there, we could pick them off one by one. And before you ask, I know just the place to lure them, the Sahara Desert. It's wide, hot, out in the open, and out of the range of any unsuspecting commoners."

"That makes sense Hope," Martha said. "The only problem is that we have no way of getting them there willingly."

Vincent smiled wide as he whipped out his sketchbook. "Who wants to bet on that?" I returned his smile, knowing exactly where he was going with this.

Chapter XVIII

I was staked outside the entrance to Area 51. I never thought that I would have been going back to the place of my "birth." In the teleport pack on my back, specially provided by Vincent, rested the almost forgotten Doomsday bomb. To my right sat Lenore, fondling her little handheld device of destruction.

"Are you nervous?"

She shot a look at me. "N-No, not nervous. Not nervous at all."

"That doesn't sound very convincing. Now, do you remember what Doomsday looks like?" She nodded. "Great, you'll do fine. Just remember not to detonate it until you see me walk out."

"Are you guys ready, yet?" Vincent asked through the device in my ear. He drew these up so that we could stay in contact. While Lenore and I were at Area 51, Natalie and Hope were at the supposed PAMNA HQ. Our main mission here was just to cause enough destruction to get them to come out into the open.

"Affirmative."

"Great. Get a move on, now. I have no idea how long you can stay in the area undetected."

"Understood, over and out."

I headed for the entrance, looking for any threats to the mission. I saw mounted missile launchers outside the main entrance. The missiles were sure to be loaded with anything left that could weaken me, so the front door was out.

I then heard a truck off to my right. Running in that direction, I saw more guards patrolling the grounds than I ever thought possible. I had to make careful use of my "Chameleon" ability to get to the loading yard.

Arriving, I found that the trucks I heard were semis. Running as fast as I possibly could, which was pretty fast, I got under the truck and held tight to the bottom. The semi took off into the garage, underwent a complete inspection, and then stopped at the loading station.

I slipped out from under it, carefully dodging the guards. I came to the door into the facility. Go figure, it was locked. No challenge for someone whose hand could change into anything he felt like. I quickly and quietly pressed my key-finger into the lock and then opened the door.

■■

After a long time of walking through twisting corridors, I ended up at the main conference room. Inside, sitting in a wheelchair, was Jonathan Tell, paralyzed from my first and only attack against him.

"I knew that you would return one day," he said, turning around in a way that faked drama.

"Everyone else may think that I've come to destroy this facility, but that can wait. I just have one question: Why was I created?"

"You can be so clueless Victor. Answer me why my only child is so disobedient."

"I'm not your child. How can you call me your child, let alone your only one? What if your daughter found out?"

"Lenore died seven years ago."

"Did she? Or are you saying it would be better if she would have died that night when you were attacked?"

"How do you know about that?"

"I have my ways."

"You want to know why you were created. Fine, I'll tell you. After the death of my family, I was attacked by another band of thieves. I fell unconscious, but not until I had seen a creature in the shape of a human come and rescue me. He was there one moment, but in a flash, he was gone again.

"I awoke in this facility, sitting in this room actually. I was instantly assigned to making the deadliest weapon ever designed, you Victor. During the creation, I gave you special characteristics that could only belong to something like you: A quick mind and a pure heart.

"During the final stages of your growth, a week before you woke up, we learned that P.A.N.M.A. had created something almost exactly like you, but in a shorter amount of time."

I stumbled back a step, knowing exactly who he was talking about. "Natalie."

"You two were created to be at each other's throats. However, we discovered that you had realized that you were the only two of your kind. Sure, there were other B.W.M.D.'s before you, but none exactly like you. You started to love each other, an outcome that shouldn't have happened.

"And now you have come back to destroy your very creators and masters."

"I have no masters. I was given a choice from the beginning: whether I would give complete control to you, or choose my own path. As you can see, I have chosen. I now know that I wasn't made only to be a weapon, but also to be a replacement."

"Oh? A replacement for whom?"

"Your daughter, Lenore Tell, who is currently listening to the entire conversation."

"Liar! Lenore is dead! Do you know how badly I want her back? But she is gone. Gone! Do you hear me?"

I reached into my pocket and brought out another ear piece. I tossed it to him, saying "Put this on."

He did, and the first thing we both heard was Lenore saying, "Daddy?" The look of shock on Jonathan's face was amazing. The very thing he had been denying was talking to him.

"Lenore?"

"Daddy, you're alive!" But her tone instantly changed from loving to hatred after that. "Is any of this true?"

Jonathan sighed. "Yes, my love, it is true. Victor was created in an attempt to recreate you, but differently."

"You mean better? Was I not good enough for you?" Her rage was evident now.

"No, Lenore. That is not at all what I meant."

"You know I have the power to kill you right now. What's stopping me from doing that?"

"Your love for him," I said.

The three of us were silent for a while. No one but I could have seen that, since I was the mediator of this debate. Eventually, Jonathan took the ear piece out and tossed it back to me. "Take me to my daughter, so I may see the young woman she has become. Also, I want to tell her in person how sorry I am for abandoning her as a child."

I nodded and, getting behind his wheelchair, I pushed out him of the room. Guards everywhere had every intention of trying to shoot me, but Jonathan put his hand up in a signal that told them to hold their fire.

We were almost out when I saw Peter. He glared at me with a look of extreme hatred. I knew that he must have somehow heard the whole thing. He knew that he wasn't part of the circle of special people like us.

Suddenly, I heard an explosion come from behind us. I knew that Lenore was close by and had detonated the bomb. I'm not sure how many the blast killed, but I'll worry about that later. Right now, I was hosting a family reunion.

When Lenore saw us, the first thing she did was drop her arm. She most likely had every intention of blowing us to bits, but then saw her father. The next thing she did was very out of character for the girl that had sought us out to find the man she was both looking for her entire life and just about to kill. She ran over and wrapped her arms around the man's neck.

"Daddy, I found you." She then broke down crying.

Jonathan lifted her head with his finger. "It's alright, Lenore. Everything is alright."

Boy, no one has ever been more wrong in ages. Right then, we were teleported out of there, into a cave where everyone else had already gotten to.

Chapter XIX

We were now in the middle of a very large desert, the battle ground for the remaining members of the warring organizations. They were scheduled to arrive in an hour or so, so I gave a quick pep talk.

"Ladies and Gentlemen, today will be the battle of battles. We are going to need everyone's individual abilities for this. Natalie and I being B.W.M.D.s. Vincent and Hope with their army of sketches. The Wolf Master with his several ghostly hounds. And Matt... What can you do, exactly?"

"I can count to potato in Einstein-ish."

"O... Kay. Anyway, everyone, just do what you're good at and this will be over before you..." I was interrupted by a bright flash of white light. Turning behind me, I saw a young man, clothed in ninja garb and holding two white swords. He wore a white head band that held up his brown hair and thin-rimmed glasses.

"Hello, father," he said with a smile on his face.

Natalie and I looked at each other, then back at him. "Who are you?" I asked.

"First, I'll answer your real question. I was based off of your design. I'm not truly your son. As for my name, it's Dos. This may sound crazy, but I am from the future."

"That actually doesn't surprise me that much. The only question is how did it happen?"

"I was testing a time portal for the King and got trapped in the vortex. I show up when needed and can't leave until I've finished the task. There is every possibility that this will wear off, but who knows after how long?"

I wanted to ask one more question, but I heard a very loud *zap!* The two armies had arrived. "Alright people, get ready. We are at war!" I walked over to Matt. "Matt, buddy, I need you to get mad, okay?"

"Okay, I'll try. But I don't think I remember how to do that."

I smiled. "I most certainly do." I walked behind him and removed the back panel of his armor, revealing a computer-like module. I wrote up a quick A.I. for Matt, and then told everyone else to back up. He instantly shot straight up like a tree and ran towards the PANMA army.

He rammed through them, knocking back the front line. He then raised his head, taking out several men during each pause in his shout, which he performed in a much lower voice than the one he had when we met. "My name is Matt H. Who. And I... Hate... Panama!"

I cupped my mouth to shout at what had become the most dangerous madman in history. "It's PAMNA., you idiot!"

"That too!" He continued ramming into the PAMNA army while I sent Vincent and Hope to help him out. The rest of us, excluding Jason, Martha, and Jonathan, ran to the other army.

The first thought that ran through my head was *Oh, great. I have to kill more people.* I was on the verge of turning around when someone shot at me. I turned in that direction, brought out my claws, and said, "Big mistake buddy." I then lashed out towards the guy, aiming right below his neck.

The blow went through him and the next five people behind him. After that, I felt a claw on my back, scrapping me and knocking me down.

The pain was almost unbearable. I then knew what it must feel like when I ran my claw into someone.

I heard another shout and rolled out of the way of another blow. I looked in the direction of my attacker. Imagine my shock when I saw it was Alpha, decked out in short sleeves and shorts, desert camouflage colored, claws on both hands, lashing at me.

He must have learned all of his abilities in a few days because most of his attacks after that were extremely clumsy. Most of them I knocked aside with little to no effort.

"What are you doing?" I yelled at him, glancing off yet another claw.

"My job."

"Can't you see that they are using you? We're nothing more than puppets if that's all we want to be. They use puppets like that."

"Shut up! What could you possibly know?"

"I know about Tia Solaris."

That knocked him off his guard. "W-Who is that?"

"I saw a list that had your name and hers. You're connected. All of us are connected."

"She was my other half. The program was created so that each of the B... we are made in pairs. Yours was never created for some reason."

"Mine was created by PAMNA," I said, barely comprehending the phrase. We were paired up from the second we became conscious? I only said that because I knew that Natalie and I were created to end the feud. I don't believe that this was the way they imagined we would do so though.

Alpha retracted his claws. "Is that so? That girl... Let me tell you, keep her safe. You come in a pair for a reason, which by now is pretty obvious. Don't let her come to any harm."

I was about to asked what he meant when I heard a screech from behind me. I flipped around to come face to face with the worst possible adversary of my kind: fifty Howlers. The equivalent of an invincible army, this high of a number meant that they were not likely to be tricked easily.

I turned back to Alpha, who nodded to me. The two of us jumped into the center of the ring. I knew that there was no possible way that the simple jump or duck trick was going to work this time. We needed to take them out ourselves.

They all inhaled slowly for a long time, a sign that showed this blow would be very fatal. Working as fast as we could, Alpha and I worked at trying to get their throats severed. We ran along the circumference of the circle seven times during our siege. The process was almost rendered impossible by the fact that something was protecting their necks. I only managed to get to one of them before I felt something lift me into the air.

Next thing I knew, I was on my back, outside the now-fallen ring of Howlers. In the middle of them was a single mangled body, the one of Peter Wily. I rushed over to him and lifted up his upper torso. "Come on, Peter. Stay with me."

His body was in total disarray. Both arms and legs were bent at odd angles. His neck was snapped to the right. Blood gushed out of his left hand and the place where his right foot once was. He opened his eyes, smiled weakly at me, then whispered, "Promise me... you'll protect...

her." His head dropped, pulse stopped. Peter Wily, the B.W.M.D. before me, was dead.

Chapter XX

I couldn't believe it. Peter Wily, Alpha to the Specials was dead. I didn't know why, but I felt a loss. It was strange, feeling this way about a man whose soul job was to destroy me. But maybe, just maybe, it was because he was like me. He was forever an outcast from the rest of mankind.

I heard the guns and other weapons being used in the background, but they were very distant. I could feel my pulse harden and quicken. I lost my breath for a second, but quickly regained it. I felt my arms scale over, like I was wearing the Reptile armor again, but it was attached to my body. For my shoulder blades, I felt two giant limbs extend. I saw the ground drop out from under me as they began moving.

What's happening? I asked in my head, expecting no answer. However, I saw images of every form of death that had been caused while I was present. The last one, the one that hung around the longest, was one of Peter and Robert, both lying on the ground, dead. I felt a gurgling in my stomach that was both hot and cold at the same time. I raised my head into the air and released a column of fire into the sky.

Looking back at the ground, I saw the faces of both organizations look in my direction. I opened my mouth to speak, but instead of words, deep growling sounds came out. This was the full potential of a Biological Weapon of Mass Destruction. This was what made me the most powerful being on the face of the Earth.

Some idiot tried firing a gun at me, but the bullet burned up on its path. I retaliated by releasing another column of fire in that direction. Twenty Area 51 members were reduced to ash in seconds.

More and more people were shooting more and bigger weapons in my direction, but to no avail. There was no stopping me. My kind was created to be the deadliest thing alive. Now, they were going to see what happened when one of them got extremely annoyed. No, not annoyed, downright enraged.

Several more were brought down, either by my fire or when I discovered that I had complete control over their weapons. There were both bodies and ashes over the sands of the desert. I was unstoppable.

The power inside of me felt amazing. I felt like I could do anything. I stirred up wind with my wings, blowing over several of the remaining soldiers. I forced up giant globs of sand, compressed it into a single stone, shattered it, and then threw it at my attackers.

Searching through the crowd of attackers, I spotted Matt on the outside, doing nothing but playing in the sand. I dashed over to him, snatched his club from him, and knocked him very far away from me. I heard a faint pop and looked in his direction, seeing nothing where he had landed.

But that didn't matter to me right now. I rose into the air, swung the club over my head, and crashed back to Earth. The impact was so massive; it created a shockwave that knocked everyone that was left back thirty feet.

After about an hour of constant attacking and destruction, I heard Natalie on the ground yelling to me. "Victor! Stop it! You've made your point."

I couldn't talk back to her normally, so I used the power of telepathy the Dream Lord gave us. Was that given for this very instant? *How can I stop, now? I have so much power!*

She spoke back in the same way. *Is that all you care about?*

They killed Peter, Natalie! They killed several people using us as puppets! We were created so that we could harness this power!

Calm down! I know that Peter was killed. I felt it also. But he did it to save you.

From an attack caused by the humans, using Howlers as puppets! How can you not be angry? Let your anger flow Natalie. Feel the power that I have now.

I saw her back glow a little and watched as two wings sprouted from her back. She flew up to me and shouted, "Listen to me! Look at what you caused!" She gestured to the blood-coated desert. "Is this what you want to be used for? Is it?"

I looked around at the destruction I had caused. What had I done? Was this the destiny the Dream Lord had foreseen for me? Is this why he told me to choose a different path?

I felt my body change back slowly into what it normally was. "No," I said in answer to her question. "This is not what I want to be."

She took my hand and led me through the bodies of the fallen. I saw Jeremy and Amelia standing over the bodies of the rest of their team. I saw Donna Sword, half limping, using her gun as a cane. I also saw numerous bodies from either team. But I saw no trace of any of the rest of ours.

"Vincent got everyone out of here when you started to change. Dos, on the other hand, disappeared half way through the battle."

I half smiled, knowing that our group was safe. But I knew that the reason that they were in any danger was me. I turned to Natalie and said, "I so sorry. I didn't know what I was doing."

She wrapped her arms around me, rocking back and forth with me as we embraced. "I know."

Suddenly, the world around us changed. We were no longer in the desert, and our group was nowhere in sight. It looked like some sort of cell. The room consisted of only two giant tubes: one labeled "Victor," the other, "Natalie."

She and I turned to face each other. "What do you think those are?" she asked.

"I have an idea, but I'm not sure how accurate it will be."

"Well, let's hear it."

"They might be holding cells. Maybe we're deemed too dangerous for the current time frame, so we were brought here as a way for waiting until the world was ready for us."

Her eyes had a sad look in them. "So, we won't be together for a long time. If that's the case..." She slammed her lips onto mine. I returned with the same amount of emotion, knowing that we won't see each other for a long time. We wanted to make this kiss count.

After what felt like half an hour, we finally broke apart and walked into our separate tubes. When we entered, they were closed tightly and filled with Acidic Mercury.

Good night, Natalie I said with our power. She returned with the same phrase. Slowly, I felt my eyes grow heavy and drift shut. I knew that soon the world would be ready for us. But until then...

■■

...We spend our days in the dream world. We sit with the Dream Lord, whose name, we learned, is Alahara, the previous king of Mora. We talk about what it will be like to walk through the woods again. What our friends will look like. And mostly, we talk about what little Alestina will grow up to be.

We learned that she is the granddaughter of Alahara. This made us even more amazed, learning that our little girl was actually the princess of Mora. I hope that she will remember us, but I know that it is a petty hope.

And to you, Reader of this story, take this to heart. Free us when the time is right. But until that day comes, live your life like you'll never see another day. Don't become like me, the B.W.M.D. Become more like those we met on our journey, friendly and compassionate. If you ever meet them, tell them that we are waiting to see them again.

Chapter XXI

We learned that she is the granddaughter of Alahara. This made us even more amazed, learning that our little girl was actually the princess of Mora. I hope that she will remember us, but I know that it is a petty hope.

And to you, Reader of this story, take this to heart. Free us when the time is right. But until that day comes, live your life like you'll never see another day. Don't become like me, the B.W.M.D. Become more like those we met on our journey, friendly and compassionate. If you have met them, tell them that we are waiting to see them again.

The young man read this bit off of the terminal with great curiosity. "'Free us when the time is right?' Well, I think the time is right now."

The boy who read this stood only a little over four feet tall. He was cloaked in a black garment, similar to that of a Howler, but he also had a mask and cape. On his side was a long black sword with a red gem in the side.

"So, you are the mythical B.W.M.D.'s that fought in the Great War. Well, your D.N.A. should do me good in making a new assistant. What Black Sword-Wielder is complete without the aid of an immortal helper?"

He looked behind him at the two creatures in the tubes floating behind him. They had been excavated and brought to him after he discovered their location. He knew that, since he was the Black Sword-Wielder, the White one wouldn't be far behind. He needed the D.N.A. of one of these creatures so he could finish his own version of them, one he called "Jamie."

"Sir," another man, older than him, said as he showed up, bowing as he spoke.

"Yes, what is it?"

"We have received word that the spirit of the Last Sword-Wielder is contained on another planet."

This was music to the boy's ears. He dismissed the man and hurried through the Morian castle. The architecture still amazed him, but he was growing more and more used to it every day. Besides, he knew the room he needed to go to.

The room was a large throne room, covered in Royal Blue and white. Though this sickened him, the king insisted on keeping his family's colors everywhere. When he was within twenty feet of the throne, he dropped to his knee and bowed his head. "Lord Bornem, Ruler of Mora."

The man-looking creature turned his head in the direction of the kneeled human. He stretched out his arm and ordered, "Arise, Hantan. You broke me out of my bondage and bestowed me with my throne. You have no need for formalities."

Hantan rose at once. "We received word that the previous Wielder has been discovered."

"You have received that word many times, and they all have been false thus far."

"True, but it had only been so because the Organization has kept it out of our reach."

"Blame not the opposition, but blame yourself. The White Organization and the Guild of Darkened Hearts. Two great empires that were built on the ruins of the stupid Earth-bound Area 51 and the mysterious PAMNA. They have been deadlocked for centuries, but I believe that this feud is coming to an end."

"And what exactly makes you think that that is happening?"

"I sense that more than one power is awakening. Your reign, along with mine, is timed by fate. We cannot change that."

"Are you certain? With the power of these two beasts we discovered, we may become unstoppable. Why do you doubt me now?"

"Because the 'beasts' of which you speak of are ready to wake up."

"That's impossible. They have been sleeping for roughly... how long?"

"Ten years."

"That means that there so-called 'Right time' could be millennia away. Trust me, Sire, I know what is best for your empire."

Without another word on the topic, Hantan walked out of the throne room. He headed in the direction of the castle's adjoined lab. It was there where his experiment was, lying in wait for its awakening.

Upon entry, he was bombarded by several Guild scientists. They were saying things like "These readings are impossible to recreate" and similar things. He ignored them all, but walked up to a young man who sat at a desk in front of a large tube. The tube contained the being that would one day become Jamie.

"You there," he said to the boy.

"Y-Yes sir?"

"What is your name?"

"It's Skink, sir."

"Ah yes, the nephew. Tell me, Skink, what do you think of these readings?" He handed him a file overflowing with papers.

Skink looked through them quickly, then answered with, "They are impossible to recreate. We've done everything we could after we got our hands on the samples, but nothing so far has worked."

"Have you tried actually, oh, I don't know, putting the samples in with him?" The fury in his voice sent half of them two the ground.

"Well, no."

"I believe that would be the problem! Who has that vile I gave them?" An older woman handed it to him. "Thank you. Now, everyone, stand back."

Hantan signaled for the top of the tube to be opened. When it had, he walked up and dumped in the contents of it. He then took a few steps back and held out his arm. *"Omega Ele Kai!"* He spoke in a tongue that wasn't quite human and not quite growling.

A beam of glowing red energy shot out of his hand, making contact with the tube. The Acidic Mercury on the inside began to glow in a similar fashion. The lights flickered around them, some actually sparking.

Suddenly, the tube began to crack slightly. Skink was the first to notice.

"Sir, the glass! It's going to break!"

Hantan turned to him; his eyes were glowing with the same color as his hands. He smiled evilly at the younger man. "You don't say? I should probably tell you that that is the plan!" He cackled as he said this last part.

Other scientist ran out of the room, others were trying to save all of their hard work. *Fools,* he thought, *they worry about their work more than their own lives. If they get out of here...*

He didn't get to finish his statement. The glass in front of him shattered almost unexpectedly. The acid splattered all over the lab, instantly killing five of the remaining scientist. Hantan, however, was immune to this, him being the Sword-Wielder and all. He simply brushed some of it from off of his mask before he looked.

Before him sat what was once the giant holding cell if his new assistant. Now, there was nothing more than a jumble of glass, acid spilling out of holes in the walls into the already nearly uninhabitable atmosphere outside.

"Jamie?" he called. There was no response at first. He was on the verge of calling the whole thing a waste of time when, out of nowhere, a claw attempted to cleave off his head. In one swift stroke, he unsheathed, swung, and replaced his blade. On the ground next to him was a large claw.

"A nice try, my friend, but still impossible." The creature who attacked him stepped out. He was tall; around six foot two, with pitch black hair. His eyes, instead of the traditional gold, were as deep as Hantan's were just moments ago.

He smiled. "So, you're the one that I'm supposed to be the second in command of."

"Second in command? No. I know that will not strike your fancy."

"Then what do you want me to think of you."

"Think of me as more of a partner. All I want is for you never to rise up against me. Ignore this, and I will assure you, it won't end nicely."

Jamie put his hand on his chin to ponder this. Then he asked, "Are there more like me?"

"No, I'm afraid." The other two had to be kept a secret from him, or he would most assuredly create more in an attempt to create his own army.

After more than half an hour, Jamie finally put his hand down. "I agree to the terms you have given me."

It was Hantan's turn to smirk now. "Perfect. Now, let us get started on going over your duties. We haven't got much time."

Chapter XXII

"Why are you keeping me here? I pose no threat to you now."

"Because killing you would have no real effect on me. Keeping you around ensures a bloodbath."

I opened my eyes slightly. The last thing I remember was going into my holding cell with Natalie going in hers. Now, I was in a prison cell, still in my tube. A few rooms over, I heard voices. Well, actually, the same voice, twice. It sounded like someone having an argument with himself.

"So, I'm being used so that you have an excuse to kill?"

"Like I need one, but yes, you are. The story goes like this: The Original Sword-Wielder splits his body. The new White Wielder gives up his power to his sweetheart. I capture him and people die trying to get him back. End of lesson. Now, if you don't mind, I have four more stones to collect.

"You're back-stabbing Bornem to get his stone?"

So, they were the same person. In a way, at least. And now, one of them is after some "stones." This whole thing was making my head hurt.

"You're so curious. Jamie! Come here and guard the prisoner!"

There was the sound of someone running down the hall. The man ran past our cell. That must have been Jamie. He seemed familiar for some reason. I just didn't know why.

"Yes, Master."

"Hopefully, this game will get more exciting as it progresses."

I heard laughter come from the man as he walked away from his prisoner. He then walked passed us, turning towards us. He wore an outfit similar to that of a Howler, but his head was incased by a black helmet and face mask.

After he continued away from our cell, I looked around the tube. It was set up exactly like the first one. I couldn't get out through the top or sides, but the bottom was perfectly fine. I easily repeated the same stunt I had the first time, but I left the bottom of the tube open. I had no idea if I had to get back in in a hurry.

After I had stretched out a little, I turned to Natalie's tube. I was working on cutting off the bottom of it when I heard a loud shout from outside. It sounded like I was back in the desert again, but that was not the case. I did, however, get back in my tube.

Using our link, I woke Natalie up. *"Natalie? Natalie!"*

I saw her stretch a little and then turn to me. She was degraded to the most basic clothing, like I was. She touched her hand to the glass before instantly drawing it back in pain.

"Be careful. You can't just walk right out."

"Where are we?"

"I don't know. This is definitely not where we went to sleep."

"Well, I got that bit. How long were we asleep?"

"I was counting the years while we slept. Twelve."

"Twelve years? We were asleep for twelve years?"

Before I could answer her, we heard an explosion happen to our left. We looked at each other, then flipped over and got out of our tanks. After we were out of our cell completely, we ran down the hall to where I heard the two that are one fighting.

After we reached the room, we stood perfectly still, hiding ourselves from all eyes. After doing so, I took in the scene.

This room was nothing more than a giant holding cell. The prisoner was in the middle, suspended in the air by ropes of energy. The boy there was just another normal person, brown hair, brown eyes, and street clothes. His head was bent down in a way that made it look like he was praying.

Then, we heard a voice come from down the hall. "Tanhan! Where are you?

The other man in the room, the one called Jamie, smirked at the boy. He then called out in the boy's voice. "I'm down here, in the cell to your left."

There was a look of alarm on the boy's face. We saw he mouth "No" several times before we saw who had called. She was a young woman, about the boy's age, with tan skin and white flowing hair. She wore a single white robe, tied off at the waist with a golden belt, a white sword hanging at her hip.

"Tanhan!" she cried in shock.

"Alice, it's a trap! Get out now!"

Jamie then used his mocking tone again. "No Alice, come and free me! I'm so helpless and desperate."

"Alice, RUN! RUN NOW!"

Alice? As in, our Alice? The little girl that we found in the woods? No, it couldn't be. But my suspicions were confirmed when I heard Jamie revert back to his normal tone to say, "Oh, no you don't! Guild of Darkened Hearts, attack! Don't let Alestina and her 'friend' get away!"

It was official. This was our Alice. I have to say I was impressed at how she looked. She became the beautiful young lady I wanted her to become. And right now, I wanted nothing more than to help her as the men and creatures clothed in black cloaks or were black themselves.

She fended them off well for a while, but she was on the verge of becoming overwhelmed when Tanhan broke his binds. He used the energy that held him up in the air as whips to get closer to Alice. Eventually, the last one was on the ground, Jamie tied to one of the walls.

After the skirmish, we watched as the two hugged tightly. After a while, Alice finally spoke. "Thank the Lord you're alive."

Tanhan smiled at her. I could see that he loved her as much as I did. "Why are you here? You have a war going on and you try to save me first? That's not usually the best move."

"Well, I couldn't just leave you here. Plus, we need more soldiers and..."

"Alice."

"And I couldn't keep your position from you so I had to give that back." She unhooked the belt from her own hip and started to hand it over to him.

He grabbed the hilt, but with it, he grabbed her hand. There was a faint glowing radiating from them. Soon, it was Tanhan wearing the robe, Alice in normal clothes. This didn't stop Tanhan from confronting her though. "Alice, tell me the truth."

She sighed. "Because I... I love you."

"Alice..." It looked like the two were about to kiss when the man in the helmet walked in. I thought that was just downright rude until I realized that evil people are usually rude in human customs. I knew that he meant more than just harm to the two.

"Ah, so keeping you captive did have more advantages than I had thought." With that, he took off his helmet and face mask.

What I saw shocked me beyond belief. I looked from this man's face, to Tanhan's, and then back again. Other than the one in black had several scars on his face and their eye color, they were absolutely the exact same.

Tanhan walked in front of Alice. "Let's end this, Hantan; right here, right now."

Hantan lifted his head and laughed. "Right now, yes, but not right here. This area is not fitting enough. What do you say we make it more... exciting."

This being said, the ground started to shake. I noticed that Hantan's eyes were as red as bloodstone now. He lifted his hands, palm down, in front of him. He then chanted something in a language that didn't register in my knowledge.

So afterwards, the floor that we had been standing on lifted up and out of the building. Carefully looking over the edges, I saw the most extensive battle imaginable. There were tens of thousands of soldiers below us. I may know very little about what was going on, but I knew that I wasn't going to enjoy the events that would take place next.

Made in the USA
Lexington, KY
09 March 2013